Sideshow

An Anthology of Freaks

Complied by Samie Sands

Sideshow

Sideshow

Sideshow

Contents

Sideshow

Panis Et Poenam
Alex Winck

"Well, even here people need some form of entertainment, you know."

Jayce couldn't find an argument against this. On the surface, his current existence couldn't look more perfect in literally every sense. He always got to wear his favorite clothes, Babolat Junior Jets: blue with yellow details, black washed out jean shorts—there was a tiny hole on the inner side of his upper thigh, but he didn't care, he loved those shorts, and a t-shirt featuring one of his favorite cartoons, *Cow and Chicken*. He also didn't care that some of his friends thought it a bad knock-off of *Ren and Stimpy* or that some adults thought it inappropriate for children, most notably an effeminate devil with exposed buttocks.

He always ate his favorite foods, always greasy, salty, sugary junk. Never had to go to school, but he had instant access to all the coolest facts that the world didn't know about, such as how you could actually make a man take flight without any machinery or where else there was intelligent life in the universe.

He could spend his days playing video games, watching cartoons, reading comics, skateboarding and skinny dipping in the lake—it was okay, no one ever saw him, even when people passed by.

But, even amidst all this non-stop loop of joy, something didn't feel right. Sometimes it'd get…repetitive. More of the same. Even things you love can wear you out if you get too much of them. So yes, even if your everyday life may look like its pure fun, you still needed a little shake-up. Even if it was simply a different form of entertainment. That was enough to light a new sparkle of excitement in Jaycee, for very simple things can fire up a ten-year-old boy, particularly Jaycee.

He was surprised to find out going to the circus was a big thing. He remembered the circus was actually a fading form of entertainment. The only one that still was a major thing in modern pop culture was that French thing, whose name he never learned how to pronounce. Even that looked a bit too artsy for him. Jaycee had to admit that old school circus was a sort of nostalgia of something he never actually had the chance to see. The magic tricks, the clowns, especially the animal tricks fascinated him. It saddened, even angered him, to find out those creatures were trained through cruel methods such as burning their paws, so much that these tricks ended up being gradually abandoned.

Still, seeing elephants as tall as houses up close, and performing as gracefully and precisely as if they knew exactly what they were doing that for, majestic and dangerous lions displaying their fangs, roaring menacingly and clawing at the solitary man ahead of them…nevermind that it was all fake, all carefully planned and rehearsed. It gave him goosebumps even though he never saw it live.

Tonight's show was indeed a major thing. It was *the* major thing, the one people talked about for days on every media, every water cooler conversation, that was, if coolers still delivered water instead of Coke or Peach Schnapps—it varied depending on the drinker. There were butts in the seats as far as Jaycee could see. He couldn't even see the walls of the circus tent, only roof as far as his eyes reached. Not even in a pop star's stadium concert, had he seen a crowd like this. His bucket of popcorn with real butter and the extra-large Coke nearly too heavy for him to carry, one hand at the verge of burning, the other nearly numb from the cold, and they were all for him. His seat was leather with heating. For a while, he could hear the usual chatting, laughing, people who couldn't wait to start loudly munching their popcorn and sucking up their bubbly drinks. But precisely on time, the lights went out, and the show began.

The host was all in red, including his bow tie, boots, and face. For a moment, Jaycee feared that this would be like that weird artsy French thing, but the host quickly set his mind at ease:

"Good night, ladies and gentlemen!" his voice a strangely unsettling mix or raspy and high-pitched, almost like nails on a blackboard. "Tonight, we present you the classic, unforgettable joys that brought you thrills and joy at the prime of your lives. This is all the fun of the old school circus, without any of the political correctness hassle. You'll see animals do wondrous, incredible things, and not a single hair of them was pulled out. You'll see magic, you'll see danger, you'll laugh and gasp at the same breath! I present you the greatest show of all!"

And the first outing, to Jaycee's delight, was taming of lions. He loved lions, tigers, all the great felines that the world immortalized on film, TV, and performances like this, yet nearly erased from the face of the Earth. Two lions and a piece of especially rare and precious beauty, a Siberian Tiger, took center of the stage, on their pedestals.

They were perfectly silent and still, consummate professionals that they were. For a moment, they're just there, and that was almost enough.

But then the tamer walked in…and it wasn't the tamer at all. It was a woman. A frail, pale, skinny woman in rags with shifting, confused, perplex eyes. No chair, no whip, not a single tool to keep the beasts at bay. Then someone else came in. An elderly, even more physically vulnerable, mostly bald man with a bit of a hunchback, a couple of cinnamon-colored spots on his forehead, suspenders holding black social pants and a bow tie. Finally, a young boy, just a few years older than Jaycee, but also wearing suspenders, shorts and a barrette that give him the vintage appearance of a late 1800's shoe shiner. He was the quietest, most stoic one of the group. If it weren't for his age, one would clearly take him for the veteran of the bunch. The three of them just stood there in front of the massive beasts. For some inexplicable reason, the crowd cheered wildly, as if the members of a chart-topping band had made their entrance.

Jayce kept waiting for the twist, for the last-minute rescue. He was sure the tamer would pop in out of the blue and save the day. They were just building up the suspense. The lions gazed at the little feast of meat delivered to them. They groaned, low at first, then it developed into a crescendo, as they exposed their bone-breaking fangs, their fur bristled, their muscles tensed up. Maybe the animals would even get a chance for a strike, enough for a scratch, to rip out another piece of the girl's already raggy clothes, and then…

The animals jumped simultaneously on them in a move with perfect synchronicity. The tiger tackled down the girl, as the lions hit the equally defenseless males. With a single bite, the boy's entire left ear disappeared and only a bloody oval was left. The tiger's claws ravaged the face of the girl, making her unrecognizable beyond the reach of any reconstructive procedure. The lion with the old man wasted no time playing with his meal. His bite engulfed the whole head of the old man, neck and all. As he pulled up, only a stump was left, bleeding like foamy gassy soda spilling out of the bottle.

You could hear the cracking of bones and squashing of flesh as the beast chewed his snack. And more.

You could hear screams. Muffled but audible screams of excruciating pain and horror echoing on the walls of those huge cheeks.

Jaycee couldn't move, couldn't speak, couldn't breathe. He couldn't even turn his eyes away, no matter how hard his brain begged his neck to move, his eyelids to shut. His hands inadvertently crushed the bag of popcorn and the cup of soda, tossing and spilling all over the place and causing neighboring audience members to grunt at him, as if that was the most bothersome event of the show so far. Jaycee couldn't process, couldn't understand, couldn't believe he was sitting at that place watching that scene. He still wanted to believe it some kind of illusion like a hyper-realistic CGI hologram or animatronic robots—did they even need that kinda thing here?

And of all places everywhere, this was the absolute last where he'd expect to see lions devouring people for an audience's entertainment.

***

Jaycee first noticed something wasn't quite right when he woke up feeling well. He hadn't felt well for about three years, which was nearly a third of your life when you're ten. He had Glioblastoma, a particularly aggressive kind of brain tumor, and inoperable in his case. Now, of course, the brain itself had no pain receptors, but the large carcinoma pressed against the surrounding blood vessels and nerves also his spinal chord, caused constant and unbearable migraines, a throb that felt like it would burst his skull open at any minute. Worse, he was part of the group of patients that didn't respond to painkillers in such a condition. He cried and screamed more high-pitched and raspier than most toddlers or even babies, he literally couldn't think of anything but the pain.

He couldn't avoid picturing himself crushing his own skull under the tires of his father's car. Just lying down there in the garage, as quiet as possible, his father wouldn't see him in the dark of the garage, he'd just reverse to take the car out of the garage and feel a bump under the car. He'd think Jaycee forgot some toy there, and as usual wouldn't have the nerve to reprehend him, until he saw what it really was.

And that was not even counting the constant, nausea, vomiting, and loss of hair from the chemotherapy. And Jaycee had lovely blonde curly hair. His mom called him "my cherubim".

What hurt worse than the tumor was not having his mother next to him to comfort him, to kiss his agonizing forehead, to tell him in her soft silky voice to never lose faith and believe God was making him go through such misery for a reason and had waiting for him a reward greater than any suffering could ever be. He'd caress the crucifix hanging from her neck like he always did, and she'd grab it along with his hand and hold them tight together. The only painkiller he needed would be to feel the natural perfume of her body, her smooth and soft skin, hold her and feel her cushion-like bosom. Of course, he knew she was beautiful, and it felt great to smell and touch her, but for a ten-year-old boy in this day and age, he was fairly innocent towards sexuality. His parents sheltered him as much as possible against inappropriate content—*Cow and Chicken* kinda slipped under their radar—and his own more sensuous feelings about that hadn't quite awakened. It just felt good, in his body and his heart, just being with her.

She was just as warm and sweet as she was severe, especially when it came to church attending, Bible reading, and sin repenting. "God always gives you a chance to repent, to plead forgiveness and, if your heart is true, he'll be endlessly merciful of your soul."

Ironically, her death was absurdly sudden. She was walking on the sidewalk, safe as can be. A driver had a sudden blood pressure drop, dozed off for a moment and lost control of his car. It hit her in the back, her head beat heavily against the hood, on which she made a dent. Her death was immediate, and she never knew what happened. At the time, Jaycee thought it was absurdly unfair, that she couldn't lie in peace in her bed, say goodbye to him and daddy, that she couldn't say her final prayers. After years of his own living Hell, he thought that actually that ending was a prime example of the endless mercy that she talked about.

Jaycee prayed, and prayed, and prayed, and repented every wrong thing he had ever done, which as one can imagine was boringly mild shit, maybe one mean prank or another, a couple days of school skipped for finely pretended diseases. He even accounted for things he only thought of, such as his suicidal fantasies, very understandable given the endless excruciating pain he was experiencing, or ideas of beating up the school bully. Even for a ten-year-old boy, it was mild, and yet he begged for forgiveness with tears in his eyes, for of course such unbearable punishment from his loving and merciful God had to match some unspeakable act.

One morning, though, Jaycee woke up, and it was all gone. No pain at all, no nausea, and his angel hair was back as if it had grown overnight. He felt warm and cheerful like never before, not even before the tumor. His dad wasn't there, instead got greeted by a couple grown-ups, all looking kinda like him with the curly hairs, but wearing togas, with halos over their heads and wings on their backs. They told him from that moment on and forever, Jaycee's existence would be one of endless joy, peace, and content. He was indeed a good boy, and all the pain and torture of the past few years would be forgotten.

But one thing never felt right. The first question Jaycee made was "where's my mom?" and they didn't answer. Not then, not the several other times he brought that up.

***

"This can't be. This is supposed to be Heaven. Why are people being tortured and torn apart? That doesn't make any sense!"

Jaycee didn't even know exactly who he was asking. He was there by himself. All his relatives who had passed away were from before he was born, they were all strangers to him. He blurted out the question out like it was meant for everyone around. What were they all doing there, cheering for that cruel and gruesome spectacle? One of the guys in togas showed up beside him, as suddenly as an old movie or TV show appear-and-disappear effect. He talked to the boy in the same gentle and smooth tone of the first time he addressed him as if nothing out of the ordinary was going on.

"Well, technically, those people over there are not really in Heaven, you see. Actually, it's quite the opposite."

It seemed obvious now that he said it out loud. Such unbelievable, surreal torture could only be a punishment from the underworld. And yet the whole situation made no sense as it presented itself.

"W—what did these people do? And why people in Heaven are watching it like it's a show? It's horrible!"

"Oh, what they did was horrible as well. The old man touched children inappropriately, and he never got caught for that, for he hid behind his frail appearance. The young lady was a model who lived for vanity, luxury, and lust, who engaged in lots of sexual acts out of marriage and abuse of illegal substances."

"And the boy?"

"Oh yes, the boy, the boy…he stole once. He was hungry, but it was a candy bar when he could have stolen an apple, so it still counted as gluttony."

Of course, Jaycee understood the notion of eternal damnation. His mother went on and on about that. The pictures of the scorching, sulfurous fire, of the hideous demons—although he thought it was kinda cool that they somewhat resembled Batman—inflicting cruel and gruesome torment to the damned was one he truly and greatly dreaded. He didn't care for his friends who said this was all make-believe, a tall tale to scare kids into early bed like the boogeyman. Okay, the devil from his beloved cartoon was different, it was a goofy caricature, more ridiculous than scary.

But right there, where he least expected, Jaycee had to watch people right in front of him suffering unimaginable torture, to a degree that wouldn't even be viable were they alive. The boy now had been torn in half, his suspenders pathetically still connected to the shorts, his lower half dangling from side to side like an unfinished string puppet as the beast, teeth deeply buried on his neck, shaken from side to side, attempting to snap the neck that bled profusely as the kid screamed a high-pitched, raspy, agonizing, terrified and furious shriek.

All this over a candy bar? Seriously?

"B—but people in Heaven sit and watch the tortures of Hell? Like it's a circus? Like a show? W—why?"

"Well, even here people need some form of entertainment, you know. Admit it, you were getting a little bored."

Jaycee didn't even get the time to absorb all this enough to express some reaction. The angel simply vanished as quickly as he had arrived, as if all he said was perfectly satisfying and he simply had more important things to do than to explain the divine machinations to some dumb kid.

As long as the endless dismemberment of the trio of sinners continued, Jaycee just sat there with his head down, trying to be too immersed in his own thoughts to pay any attention to the agonizing and nauseating sounds as the lions were now munching on organs, muscles and fat, and cracking bones for the marrow inside. Although they still saw days passing in Heaven, one could easily drop the notion of time once they didn't have any responsibilities that demanded a schedule. But his residual living memory of it gave him the impression that the spectacle went on for hours. When it was finally over, the crowd gave it a standing ovation full of shouting and whistling. Jaycee's parents only took him to see one concert by gospel singer Koryn Hawthorne, and it didn't come anywhere near that level of excitement. Probably not even Heavy Metal shows loaded with headbanging fans matched up.

Jaycee just remained seated there in absolute silence. He couldn't even hear the sound of his breathing, for, of course, that was no longer a necessity. On one hand, the mostly full bucket of popcorn went cold. On the other, the soda became warm.

**

Jaycee pondered if he shouldn't just stand up and leave. Spare himself from watching any more horrors. Refuse to take part in this sadistic and clearly blasphemous charade.

But no. This had to be it. It must be the Heaven his mother told him so many times about. The signs were all there. Remember, mysterious ways. As horrendous as it looked, this must, somehow, have a place in the divine design. He stayed in his seat, although the bucket and cup now slipped to the side, nearly full.

The next attraction was announced:

"Now was that a tasty treat or what, ladies and gentlemen?"

More cheering accompanied by bursts of laughter.

"Well, after starting with such a bang, now is time for something softer and lighter, I'd say. After a jolt of adrenaline, nothing like some laughter to relieve the nerves, wouldn't you agree? Ladies and gentlemen let's hear it for Belial The Clown!"

And the crowd went wild again. Apparently, this was a big star around. Personally, Jaycee, like most kids, thought clowns were lame and unfunny. Not to mention more than a little creepy.

As Belial entered the stage, Jaycee pictured if Heath Ledger's Joker and Pennywise from *It* had a baby, that baby would find the clown terrifying. It had Joker's black make up around the eyes, but they were unnaturally round with tiny pupils, no iris, that bring up an air of supernatural dementia. The smile, way too large, almost like a crocodile's mouth, pointy, crooked, also like a crocodile, the nose was red but not a ball and more like a beaky witch nose, the classic pale skin with crimson sores, the hair hot red and straggly like a bleeding bush. His bow tie overly large and black, suspenders—again, what's with so many suspenders?—for overly large parachute pants that would look right only in an old MC Hammer video. He had this flower on his lapel, looked more like a big mouth with pointy teeth like his own, resembled those flesh-eating plants that gulped down a fly like a cage closing. His jacket was hot pink, and pants were full bright yellow, yet everything about him felt dark and menacing.

He was joined by a man. One would think it'd be another clown, but he was wearing a gray suit with a black tie. His face was square and hard, like a piece of granite carved with a pickaxe, black hair with grey sideburns, a general air of severity like those loudmouth cranky bosses from old movies and TV shows. At least six-five feet tall, broad shoulders, he would be just as intimidating if he was wearing a Hawaiian flowery t-shirt and cargo pants.

But then he smiled. And suddenly the clown looked as menacing as a feather in the wind. A toothless smirk that, along with his hollow, expressionless gaze, made him feel like a ghoul, like the closest thing to a demon without horns, tail, fangs or claws.

Sideshow

"Good night, ladies and gentlemen. May I introduce you to my stage partner, mister Jimmy Hanks. Now you may not recognize him because he lived anonymously. But those of you alive in the 1970's certainly heard of his accomplishments."

He approached Jimmy Hanks and pointed him the microphone.

"Good night, Mister Hanks. Now, how do you like my wardrobe for this show?"

The man spoke with that voice that nobody had anymore, that cavernous raspy, ground voice of people who smoke ten packs of unfiltered cigarettes and drank five bottles of bourbon a day through the course of a long life.

"Yes. Quite stylish."

Belial now pointed back the mic to himself.

"Isn't my flower beautiful? Would you like to smell it?"

"Oh, absolutely!" he replied now showing his teeth, and it was like a dog whose plate of food was taken away in the middle of his meal.

Usually, Jaycee would sigh with impatience and roll his eyes. The oldest, most cliché clown gag in the world. But here, his heart skipped a beat and he clenched both his bucket of popcorn and his cup of soda, that he simply didn't bother to throw away.

So, Jimmy Hanks leaned to smell the flower, and of course, he was in the joke. Belial didn't even need to squeeze the flower, it just spit it out right away. At first, the liquid looked like water, as in the traditional trick, but then a puff of smoke rose from Jimmy's face with a hissing sound and he screamed in his ground voice, such a bad flu scream in his smoker, drinker voice, and yet deafeningly loud. It was darkly funny when Joker did that in the first

Tim Burton *Batman* movie, but in this version, he saw the man's face sink and dissolve into muscles, nerves, and tendons and then he got a clear sight of his cheekbone under his left eye. Again, the crowd went ape-shit. The clown laughed uproariously in a high-pitched hyena-like shriek, and everyone but Jaycee cackled along. Then he just turned to the audience like a magician adding context to his trick.

"That's right, ladies and gentlemen. This is the famous Face Burner killer who terrorized Illinois in the 1970's. Met young, beautiful women, lured them into his van with various excuses, and melted their faces with acid before sodomizing them and eating pieces of their bodies while still alive. Isn't that true, Jimmy?"

His face still bubbled as the killer caught his breath and grabbed the mic from the clown as if nothing had happened. He smiled again.

"You're damn right, Belial. I confessed thirteen killings, but I actually killed thirty-three lovely ladies."

He said that with a sense of pride too, like they handed him trophies for that, not damned him to be the butt of a sadistic joke forever. Belial grabbed the mic back.

"Why did you do it? Because you were traumatized? Molested, abused?"

"Because I loved it. Since I was a kid, I knew that was the kind of thing I was cut out for. Even in damnation, I feel like this was God's plan for me."

"You don't regret it for a moment, do you? Even after years of damnation?"

"I've experienced pain and suffering like no living being could bear. Every moment of my existence is agony. And yet…and yet…I still feel the rich metallic flavor of their hearts in my mouth."

"Oh, speaking of eating…"

Then he turned to his show sidekick and the acid-spitting plant simply popped out of his jacket and grabbed his nose. Immediately blood cascaded down his mouth and chin. His scream now lower and muffled, like someone wearing a clothespin on his nose, not a rose-shaped piranha. For a moment, Jayce almost found actual humor in that and nearly mumbled a little chuckle. The thing just kept biting away nonstop all over him. He fell down to the floor, trying to push it out unsuccessfully.

"Well I don't have a whole swarm of those suckers to finish this under a minute, so this is gonna take a little while. You all wanna see the whole banquet?"

Again, a standing ovation.

But this time, Jaycee almost felt like joining it.

It was still all very cruel and horrible, but this was such a horrible and cruel man as well. To hear that, even in his torment, he still relished in the unspeakable acts he committed…

The fact that Jaycee wasn't raised on a diet of psycho killer movies and news stories only made it even more appalling to hear those words. It was painful for Jaycee to think any human being might deserve such a destiny, but if anyone did, that would be Jimmy Hanks. This particular act warmed him up a notch about the whole bloodfest. Were it up to him to make the call, Jaycee couldn't say he would have been any more merciful.

***

Jaycee knew watching the rest of this evening's entertainment wouldn't be an easy task, but then again nothing about being true to your faith was. Not even enjoying your eternal reward, apparently.

Once again, the announcer made the call for the next show.

"This has been a magical night indeed, and it's about to get even more magical. Remember how disappointed you were to find out how a magic trick was done? To see that seemingly impossible and inexplicable achievements turn out to be nothing but smoke, mirrors, trap doors? Well, here there's no place for that. Here, all really is possible, all one imagines and desires. And our next attraction has imagined great things for your appreciation. Welcome, The Great Asmodeus!"

A puff of maroon smoke blew on stage. One would expect the magician to show up behind it, but instead, the smoke formed into the silhouette of his body solidified, changing color and formed his body. It was like watching a visual FX but performed live.

Asmodeus, in fact, looked like a typical stage magician, with a pointy goatee, wearing a tuxedo and a top hat. He took the hat off for a bow and two little horns on his head were exposed.

"Allow me to introduce my beautiful stage assistant."

Indeed, she was beautiful. Curvier than usual, but still in good shape, with thick strong thighs exposed by her swimsuit-like black outfit, her genre sumptuous bosom nearly bursting out of the cleavage, sexy electric blue eyes, and curly blonde hair.

Jaycee's mother.

In a way, Jaycee hadn't felt this alive in a long time. He nearly forgot he had a heart, and now it pounded and bounced in his chest, never taking a breath. His chest rapidly inflated and deflated like in a race. He also felt like he was about to die, even though that was currently impossible.

Now he knew for sure this was all wrong. Of all people on Earth, dead or alive, his mother would never be in Hell. And if she was not in Heaven, nobody should be. Look at her, nervous, shaking, staring down, avoiding the accusing eyes of the crowd. That was nothing like her. She strutted around chin up wherever she went. This fraud needed to be stopped.

Jaycee stood up and ran towards the stage. He had absolutely no idea what he was gonna do once he got there, but it didn't matter. If he truly deserved to be raptured, there must be something he could do for her. Even if there wasn't, he would still find a way.

But as soon as he got to the edge of the stage, his sprint simply halted. He couldn't move any further, frozen in his running position. The boy managed to take a step back. He remembered what the angel said, technically the stage was a piece of Hell. As an inhabitant of Heaven, crossing over to the opposite side would be trespassing.

And of course, the show just kept going as this ensued.

The magician took a rope, pulled her hands to her back and tied her wrists together.

"I'll tie her up firmly, so there's no way for her to escape."

He pointed theatrically to the floor as a stake rose from it, right between her back and her wrists. It simply grew out of the floor much like T-1000 coming out of the kitchen floor. She breathed hard, pale, but didn't utter a single word of pleading for her eternal soul. The magician continued his set up, completely ignoring her agony as if she were all smiles and pantomime gestures.

"As you can see, she looks prepared for what will certainly be a mind-blowing magic trick..."

He pointed again to the floor with a quick gesture, like dropping something, although his hand was seemingly empty, then a puff of smoke rose right under her, and like the magician did before, the amorph gas regrouped and shaped into a bunch of logs under her feet.

"Which is why she shall burn at the stake for taking part in an act of witchcraft, am I right?"

The crowd responded with its usual gusto and glee while Jaycee gritted his teeth. He kept pushing his body forward, yet his muscles simply refused to move forward.

That was when he recalled something. His mother's crucifix.

He kept it to himself after her passing, as both a memento of her, which still exhaled a bit of her scent and also to empower his prayers. In Heaven, he still had it in his pocket. He pulled it out and contemplated it. Now, his mother made it clear that the supposed biblical passage where Jesus descended to Hell and took its keys from Satan was just a popular myth, a thing from movies and comic books, that it was not in the Bible at all. In fact, it annoyed her greatly that so many believed in it. "No one goes to Hell right now, that's for judgment day," she used to say. Well, if that is true, that day had arrived already. And if anyone could really cross over to Hell and back, that would be Jesus. The crucifix was a symbol to Christ, and if there was a place where symbols held real power, it was this.

Jaycee clenched it as if his mother's hand was over his once again, and he summoned the power of Christ to compel him into the stage.

Sideshow

The magician snapped, and a flame, like that of a Zippo, rose from his fingers. He made a curvy move with his hand that sent the fire like water spilling towards the logs. They lit up under his mother's feet. On top of the heat and smoke, it exhales the unmistakable sulfur of Hellfire.

With all of his focus and all of his faith, Jaycee walked into the stage.

And the crowd and magician and his mother all gasped in astonishment. For a moment, the loud event became deadly silence. One could only hear Jayce's quick steps, in synch with the creaking of burning wood.

"*Stop*!" he yelled desperately and furiously. "Put out that fire. Stop, please!"

Even the demonic magician stared in stunned disbelief for a moment, not quite sure of how to react. This was too out of the ordinary for him to absorb and process, even though he was billions of years old.

His mother, on the other hand, stared in horror, eyes wide, trembling lips. She wanted to scream, but the sound suffocated in her throat. Completely a passive accessory to her own inquisition as she desperately tried to squeeze her wrists out of the rope's grip, hopeless as that effort was.

Appalled, the demon illusionist must agree this was too much of a disruption for the performance to simply continue business as usual. He pointed his hand to the fire and it halted like a paused movie, the flames unmovable. And yet, she could still feel the intense heat on her feet, the stench of burnt leather from her high heels beginning to melt mixing with the sulfur and suffocating smoke.

"Wha—what's wrong with you, kid? It's highly blasphemous to cross from Heaven to infernal ground. It's not even technically possible far as I know."

"She's innocent! She doesn't deserve damnation."

Only now his mother mustered the strength to yell as loudly as she could.

"Jaycee, please, get out of here! You can't be here. There's nothing you can do for me."

"That she's right about, boy," agreed Asmodeus. "Her destiny has been sealed by her own doing."

"That woman is my mother! She taught me faith, taught me to love Jesus, taught me right from wrong," Jaycee insisted, struggling to keep his voice firm between sobs and heavy breaths. "What could she have possibly done to deserve the tortures of Hell?"

That was when she finally burst into desperate tears, for the first time since she learned of her destiny. Burning in eternal flames was nothing compared to seeing her boy's innocence and confidence in her betrayed before his very eyes. The one punishment she expected to dodge was to make him suffer for her mistake, her sin.

The magician smiled in a way that made Jaycee's skin crawl.

"Well, well, well, we were getting to that part of the show anyway. I mean, the whole witchcraft thing was more for theatrics, you know. Care to explain to your adoring, faithful son why you're here and not there with him, Mrs.—"

"No! Please don't make me say it!"

"You're not really asking for mercy in Hell, are you? Well, if you don't, I will. And I won't miss any of the sordid details. Besides, the boy went from Heaven to Hell for you. The least he deserves is to know why."

She lowered her head, now completely oblivious to the heat under her feet. Her voice came out strangled, barely audible.

"I…I cheated on my husband. With a stranger."

Sideshow

Jaycee didn't have a reaction to that revelation. It was like he didn't even hear it. His mind couldn't absorb, couldn't process that information. She couldn't have said that…could she?

"C'mon. You can elaborate a little more than that," teased Asmodeus. "You can just skip the graphic stuff."

She looked around. The crowd that so far laughed and cheered their hearts out now remained in stunned silence. You could hear their breaths if they still needed to breathe. Still, as a purely emotional gesture, she took a deep breath before proceeding with her narrative.

"It happened inside an elevator. It was a really old one, had no surveillance camera. A man got in next to me. He was working on repairs to the building I worked in. He wasn't even a particularly handsome man, he was this hairy and sweaty Latino guy wearing dusty gloves. But maybe that was it, a raw masculine charm, I dunno. I have no idea what came over me, it was completely not like me to do something like that, completely impulsive. I had never been with any man other than my husband. Maybe it was all the years of self-repression. Maybe it was just too good a chance to pass, whatever. The elevator broke, we got stuck in there for a while… We had…and we had sex."

Jaycee didn't know if his heart was more broken for himself, to his surprise and disappointment, or more for her. He knew her heart, he knew keeping a secret like that would have torn her soul apart more than any bonfire possibly could.

"'Had sex? That's dreadfully modest of you, dear!" chuckled Asmodeus. "The elevator got stuck for about half an hour. You did things to him you'd certainly never ever do to your hubby, didn—"

"Enough," she yelled now with a hint of righteous fury. "You don't have to spare me, but at least spare him. He's an innocent! He's from Heaven. Certainly, none of my sins are his fault."

"Fair enough. Now that all is clear, allow me to continue, show must go on and all that."

He pressed the "play" once again to the fire, that advanced further towards her feet. She just closed her eyes, ready to take it all in.

But Jaycee was not. Those flames burned right into his heart. He just knew it wasn't the way it was supposed to end for her.

"Wait," yelled Jaycee. "Mom, you always told me that if you repented your sin, sincerely, God would show you endless mercy. Of course, you did repent it!"

She hoped that the fire would just completely swallow her now and burn down her tongue. But it was like he said, there's no mercy in Hell.

"I…I didn't. I mean, not fully. Not wholeheartedly. I struggled for a long time with the guilt, yes, but also a part of me…a part of me really liked to be bold, to dare, to break the rules. I had fantasies of doing something like that again, sometimes…sometimes even in bed with your father. You know, Father Merrin told me to do an act of contrition, to tell your father the truth and plead for forgiveness. But I couldn't. I just couldn't. I knew he'd divorce me right away. And there's no way I could live with that. With all I had done, I still loved him. And the two of you were the best of friends. I could never do anything that'd separate you, not even shared custody."

And now the tears really streamed down her face, she could hardly breathe enough to let the next words come out.

"And God knows I could stand it even less to be separated from you. My Hell started the day I realized I would never see you again."

She couldn't bear to look in his eyes. She lowered her head and faced the fire.

"And yet now that I do, all I wish is I didn't."

Somehow, it was even more appalling for Jaycee to hear that admission from her than the psycho killer's proud speech. Jimmy Hanks was a monster all around, that was simply who he was. For a boy who still retained much of a genuine childhood innocence, to realize that someone as kind and pure of heart as his own mother could not only do wrong but still crave it, still desire that dark satisfaction, guilt and all, seemed inexplicable. And most of all deeply painful.

Now Asmodeus really sighed and waved impatiently to the boy.

"Well? There you go, kid. She's your mommy and you love her, but she fucked up. She's damned fair and square, that's how this whole system rolls. Life's a bitch, and so's afterlife. Can I get this over with if you don't mind?"

For a moment, Jaycee just stood there, as the flames took their first licks of her feet. No one said a word, not even the demonic magician. The audience just watched, now unsure of their feelings. Only the fire kept on crackling wood, leather, and began to hit skin.

But then he clenched hard the cross in his hand, until the corners hurt his skin. He shot a look at Asmodeus and pointed him the cross like he saw people do to vampires in movies.

"Go away!"

The demon sighed exasperatedly. He'd had it with this kid already.

"No, Jaycee," yelled his mother in agony. "There's nothing you can do for me. Get away. Go back!"

"C'mon, kid. Who you think you are, an exorcist? It's not that eas—"

Actually, that gave Jaycee an idea. "The power of Christ compels you! The power of Christ compels you! The power of Christ compels you!"

Asmodeus giggled at first, but it did compel him. He couldn't resist an urge to step back as the kid kept walking towards him and the burning stake.

Jaycee approached the flames. The heat was so intense he could barely stand to be a couple of yards from it. He focused completely on the glow of the cross.

"Okay, hope this doesn't work and as he píconly on water," he thought to himself.

And as he pictured it, the flames opened from center to the sides and made a small trail for him to pass through.

"Stop, Jaycee, please," begged his teary mother. "It's too late for me. You may get yourself in trouble for this."

"She's right, kid," supported Asmodeus. "What's done is done. She can't be saved anymore."

Ignoring them, Jaycee simply walked around her, trying not to trip on the logs, and began to untie her.

"She raised a son who will leave Heaven, go down to Hell, and face the fire to rescue her. If that woman's not worthy of salvation, who is?"

Neither she nor Asmodeus had a proper response for that. He finished untying her, and tightly held her hand with the same one that held the crucifix. She stared into his eyes with the saddest smile he'd ever seen and clenched his hand like she did back in the world of the living.

They walked towards the edge of the stage. One member of the crowd slowly began to clap, then another, and soon everyone in the circus was cheering for them. A redemption like no one had ever seen before. A happy ending in Hell…

But that was when the same angel who had half-heartedly explained the concept of the circus to Jaycee showed up on stage, and now he pointed a flaming sword to the boy and his mother.

"*Halt*!"

Once again Jaycee was reminded he still had a heart, for he felt a tight grip to it, as tight as his mother's own grip of his hand. Deep down, she knew there was no way this could end well.

The angel's eyes went fully white, and his voice became even more commanding and intimidating, the sound of thunder with words.

"The Lord your God speaks!"

Everyone around, even the demon, shared a collective gasp, and goosebumps. Even beyond the physical world, they would never see or hear God in person. Even if He was speaking through an angel, that spelled major trouble.

Even so, Jaycee still summoned strength in himself to question Him.

"If you're really God…what's the point of all this? Why must people in Heaven enjoy themselves watching torture and violence?"

"People, even the kindest, have always enjoyed watching punishment. When Romans watched Christians being devoured by lions, they believed the Christians were in the wrong, they believed the Empire's lies that eating the body and drinking the blood of Christ in the last supper was literally cannibalism, among other things. Then Christians watched sinners and Pagans being burned and hanged. In recent times they've watched criminals being electrocuted, asphyxiated by gas or poisoned. People enjoy more to watch evil punished than good rewarded. For the audience, the movie doesn't end when the hero kisses the girl, it ends when the villain falls down the cliff. People here may not need bread anymore, but they still need a circus."

"But, like with the Christians and the lions, a lot of those times people turn out to be innocent."

"That's okay Jaycee," insisted his mother, a feeling of dread tingling more and more in her no longer necessary gut. "That is the flawed justice of men. Here, is applied divine justice."

"Look, my mother's not perfect, but who is? She has her demons, we all do. She's a good person, she doesn't deserve this. She sure doesn't belong in the same place as fu—, as Jimmy Hanks!"

"Only I can be the judge of that. She is damned, Jaycee…and so are you."

"*No*!" Jaycee's mother yelled so loud the crowd got about as big a jump scare as when they heard God's voice. "He's got nothing to do with what I did! He's just a son who wanted to help his mother, there's nothing wrong with that. You sent him to Heaven, you judged his soul already."

"Even a soul in Heaven still has free will. He attempted to take a justly condemned soul out of Hell, to violate the divine plan."

The audience had absolutely no reaction. Even if they had doubts about that decision, no one dared to challenge it. That could also come off as a violation of the plan.

"The Lord has spoken," the angel now said in his regular voice and disappeared.

Sideshow

The boy didn't feel the crucifix in his hand anymore. He opened his palm, and it was gone.

His mother knelt down in front of him, her face all wrinkled and twisted with tears. But he smiled at her, just the way he always did.

"My boy, my boy…what did I do to you? I cost you Heaven!"

"No, mom. This place…this place is a fraud. Whatever it is, a place where people enjoy watching others suffer…that place could never really be Heaven."

She held his cheeks, still trying to figure out the inexplicable peace she saw in his eyes.

"Because of me, your immortal soul will spend all eternity in Hell! That's the worst thing a mother has ever done to a son."

Now his smile was all teeth.

"If you're there, Mom, no place could really be Hell."

And he held her as tight as he ever had. The flames swallowed them whole. But he sunk in her cushion-like, silky, warm embrace, he couldn't feel the scorching abrasive heat, and her natural perfume erased the stench of sulfur.

Alex Winck

Alex Winck was born on February 16, 1974, at Blumenau, Brazil. Graduated in Social Communications and Journalism. Is a writer, journalist, editor, translator (English-Portuguese). Wrote nearly 100 issues of Sesinho, Brazil's most popular educational comic book for children, with nearly one million copies distributed for free in schools, monthly.

Currently writes for the Brazilian superhero comic book project Sunburn, which includes several characters. Has had several short horror, fantasy and sci-fi stories published in anthologies compiles by author Samie Sands, including the latest one, "Doomsday".

Make My Escape
C.L. Williams

I wake up and realize I'm tied to a chair. I cannot move, I cannot see. I notice not only am I tied to a chair, I'm also blindfolded. I try to move, I feel something shock me. It was painful enough that I stopped making any movements, that is until someone or something untied me and grabbed me.

I feel something underneath my feet vibrate. Whatever it is I'm both hearing and feeling, is coming closer in my direction. I do my best to stay still. I'm not sure if I'm being freed, or if I am about to be killed. I feel something near me, I think who, or what is planning to kill me. Instead, I am being cut free from the chair I'm bound to. Whoever it is that has untied me, is not picking me up and putting me over its shoulder. I'm being treated like a ragdoll as I am being carried somewhere else.

The cover is removed from my head and it's revealed I was taken by a clown the size of a linebacker. He puts his finger over his mouth, I'm guessing this means he wants me to keep silent. He then goes to the door in front of me and hits the door. Given his size, I'm guessing this is his way of knocking. After he hits the door, a maniacal clown comes in and prances his way to me. After he is done prancing, he hits me in the stomach, then he introduces himself.

"HELLLLLLLLLLLOOOOO JERRY!" the clown says in much excitement. "Tonight! WE will be playing a game. I love games! Do you love games, Jerry?" I don't answer because he doesn't give me enough time to answer him. "OF COURSE

Sideshow

YOU DO! This game is simple. I let you loose throughout the carnival. My friends will try to kill you. Survive, and we'll let you go! If we get you," his voice then goes from happy to demonic, "we will end your life without hesitation. Are we clear?" I nod my head in agreement to this psycho clown. "Good, then you are free to go! Good luck Jerry!"

After he tells me good luck, he and the large clown then leave the room from a different door. I go through the door the large clown attacked earlier. As I am leaving, I look at the door and notice this is, or was, the office for whomever once ran this circus. I look around me as I am making my way to the circus grounds hoping to see if there's a way to escape this place and avoid being killed by a group of clowns of all things. I'm not seeing anything, which means I'll have to play their games, for now at least.

As I am exiting this hallway, I notice myself walking into a dead end. I then realize the game has already begun. I was told I'm at a carnival and here I am already stuck in the maze. If I get caught, that means a clown could come and find me and possibly kill me. I start pushing the walls, hoping for a secret exit from this maze. I don't find a secret in the wall, but I do find a trap door and I quickly fall through.

As I am falling, I eventually end up on a slide, my momentum is too fast for me to stop myself, or even look for possible ways out. My only option is to keep sliding until I hit the bottom, wherever the bottom of this slide may be at. I take a chance and do my best to stop myself on the slide and see if there's a way off or a way out. I burn my hands trying to stop myself from sliding down and I let out a scream I know the clowns can hear. As I am screaming in pain from burning my hands, I eventually make my way to the bottom of the slide. I fall into a boat that's about three feet below the bottom of the slide. I don't have time to catch myself as I notice I'm on one side and there's another boat with a clown in it on the other side.

Sideshow

"Hiya Jerry! Are you READY TO DIE!" the clown says as he is laughing hysterically.

I'm not exactly able to respond. Between burning my hands on the slide and the unexpected drop from the slide to the boat, I was in too much pain to really respond to his threats and his taunts. After he asked me if I was ready to die, I tuned him out and I don't remember anything else he said. As he is taunting me and running his mouth, the boats begin moving. He shuts up and just stands there on his boat and laughs at me. I'm not sure why he is laughing, my guess is he is trying to play mind games with me. As we are going through this water, the boats go faster. I went from being slightly dazed due to my fall from slide to boat, but now I've sunken myself into this boat and I'm holding on for my life.

He keeps laughing at me, taunting me, trying to make me scream. I see him pointing straight ahead and he begins laughing. I raise myself up to see what's ahead and I can see why he is now laughing at me. My boat is not far from hitting a cement wall and his boat will continue going down the stream. I only have two options; jump to the walking area to my right or jump to the left and be on the same boat as the clown. The clown who told me what is going on told me that these clowns intend to kill me if I don't make my escape from this place. Jumping onto his boat would not be a good idea for me. As the adrenaline hits me, I take a leap and end up on the walking area next to the boat. I watch the clown leave as he continues to laugh at me and I see my boat run into the cement, destroying the boat in the process.

I look at my arm and notice I have scraped myself. I see blood dripping onto the hard concrete I landed on. I don't exactly have anything I can use to clean myself up. The water is dirty and likely hasn't been cleaned recently. If I use that to clean myself, I'll likely cause an infection. I do my best to get myself up and hope that there is an easy way out of the area I'm currently in.

Sideshow

As I am walking, I see light. Given I was taken in the dark I'm clearly looking at a way out of this area. I follow the light and I have two choices in front of me. I can either go to the Ferris Wheel set up to my left, or I can go to the haunted house to the right. I make my way to the haunted house as I feel they'll likely stop the Ferris Wheel or keep me strapped in, that way they can kill me easier.

As I am making my way to the haunted house, I see a kid. At first, I think it's a kid who somehow got lost. Then I see the kid turn around and reveal he's wearing clown make-up.

"Hi, Jerry. Are you ready to die?" the kid says in a creepy voice like that from a horror film.

"You're too young to be here," I tell the kid. He then reveals something in his hand and uses it to cut my leg. While it didn't do severe damage, it was enough for me to bleed once more. I can't do much because I have nowhere to go. Once I entered the haunted house, the doors were shut behind me immediately. I have to go through the haunted house, or I could possibly lose my life. As I am making my way through the house, the clown who kidnapped me makes his presence known.

"HEELLLLLLOOOOOOOOOOOOO JERRY! I see you made it to the haunted house." He then goes into his demonic voice, "I have some friends who are DYING to meet you!"

The second he says they are dying to meet me; two clowns reveal themselves and attempt to attack me. I'm not sure what I did or how I did it. But, I managed to evade the attack. The two clowns are still coming after me. I run down the hallway and find the stairs leading to the second floor of the haunted house. As I am making my way up the stairs, the head clown makes his presence known once more.

"Jerry," he says in a sad voice, "my friends want to play with you and they can't do that if you run from them." He then goes from sad to demonic, "Looks like I, yes ME will have to change that!"

I don't know exactly what he's doing but the stairs I'm on suddenly turn into a slide and I am on my way down to two killer clowns who want to kill me. I grab the banister before I can be victims of whatever sadistic plans these two devil clowns have in store for me. I hold on to the banister and slowly climb to the top of the transformed stairs and look for a way out.

I see the head clown has turned the transforming stairs back into stairs. Meaning the two devil clowns at the bottom of the staircase are on their way, ready to kill me if they get a chance. I run down the hall and discover every door I come to is locked. I find one unlocked door and make my way in the room. I see a closet and run inside before the two devil clowns can come after me. I slowly close the door to avoid it making any noises, that way I don't attract them to my location. I sit in the closet and wait for them to pass by this room. As I am in the closet I hear something.

"Are you ready to die?" is whispered in my ear followed by whoever it is licking my face. I immediately run out of the closet and another clown reveals herself. She then licks her lips after licking my face, "My, my, Jerry. You taste delicious! I'll eat you after I KILL YOU!"

She then reveals an ax behind her and is about to hit me before I roll out of the way. After she yelled, her yelling brought in the two devil clowns who were trying to attack me earlier. As I see the two devil clowns come in, I come up with a plan that might work in my favor. Before the bigger of the two can attack me, I make a move of desperation. I kick him in the balls. He screams and falls within seconds. This angers the other devil clown, he comes running towards me, knife in hand. Given it worked once, I try it again. I also kick him in the balls, as he hunches over, I manage to trip him, and he falls. He lands on his knife, possibly killing him.

Seeing he may possibly be dead, the woman with the ax comes running after me wanting to get vengeance for what I may have possibly done to her cohort. Knowing my move of desperation will be of no use here, I crawl my way to the door and out of the room. I use the knowledge to get myself back on my feet and I close the door before she can make her attack. It was close given the ax blade was sticking out of the door once I closed the door.

I'm in the hallway once more, limping my way to any possible exit I can find in this haunted house. I see the giant clown who I first encountered when I first regained consciousness, he's not slowly making his way towards me, he's running! For a person of his size, he's incredibly fast too. I have no other choice, to avoid him killing me, I go back to the stairs that's a slide once more and slide my way back to the first floor. He just stands at the top staring at me. He shows no emotion, but that blank face of his is something that will give me nightmares for years to come. As I am on the floor I notice something, I see a glimmer of light peeking its way inside. I know it's dark outside, so I'm not sure where this light is leading. I know I have to find out where. I have a mammoth of a human being, a psycho clown, and a devil clown ready to kill me. I need out of here.

I see a chair and I use it to break whatever is keeping the light from coming into this room. After hitting the wall a few times, I finally manage to let more light enter this room. It's a security light that's located in front of the haunted house. I am back on the porch once again, this time no little kid ready to stab me, the mammoth clown cannot fit through the opening I made. As far as the psycho clown and the living devil clown, I'm not sure if they will come after me or not.

Now that I am on my feet once more, I look around and notice something I didn't notice before. The Ferris Wheel is lit up and operational. Given it was only lit up when I first saw it, I guess there is something, or someone waiting for me there. I limp my way to the Ferris Wheel and see if I am correct about my assumptions.

I make my way to the Ferris Wheel and none other than the head clown is now standing in visible sight of me. He looks eager to be face to face with me. The look of deranged happiness upon his face as I make my way to him and hopefully my escape from this place. I make my way to him and he is making his way to me. As I notice he is walking towards me, I begin to run towards him. He gets excited as I am running because he goes from walking to briefly skipping, to running in my direction. As I get closer I get ready to punch him, but he's prepared. As I am running with my fist ready to hit him, he trips me, and I fall on my injured leg. I'm now on the ground screaming while he happily prances around me, giggling at making me fall to the ground.

"Poor Jerry, but good for ME! I'm going to win!" he says as he prances around my fallen body. As he prances, he occasionally kicks me, making sure I stay on the ground. He then begins a monologue. "When I first grabbed you, I knew you'd be FUN to play with! I thought you'd do more than what you did, but oh well. I'm still getting what I want!" He then goes into his sinister tone for a moment, "I did not appreciate you kicking my friends in their jewels and I most certainly DESPISED you killing one of my dear clowns." He then goes back to his happy tone. "That requires you being killed!"

Before he took his knife or gun out, I make a small attempt to stall him. I know nothing may come of this, but I try it anyway. "I have to ask one question. Before you kill me, I need to know one thing. You took me. There are killers, rapists, thieves, all kinds of people out there and you took me. I want to know why! Why did you take me?"

"It's simple Jerry." He then moves closer towards me and whispers into my ear. "You were home and left your doors unlocked!"

He then stabs me and prances around me as I slowly lose consciousness.

***

I wake up with a light shining in my eyes. I'm sitting on something hard and cold. I soon realize the light is being held by what looks like a paramedic. She tells the other person I'm alive and awake. She then looks at me and begins asking me questions.

"Are you ok? Can you breathe with no difficulties? Do we need to keep you overnight?"

I tell her I was stabbed by a clown who intended to kill me and a trip to the hospital is probably the best option I have at the moment.

She then tells the driver I'm awake and to start driving. I'm not sure if I'm delusional from my night around the clowns or not but as we're moving I'm not hearing sirens, I'm hearing the sound of an ice cream truck. I then look to see a picture of an ice cream sandwich on the wall in front of me. I pass out before I can say or do anything.

C.L. Williams

C.L. Williams is an independent author from central Virginia. Over the last few years C.L. Williams has written and published poetry, horror, fantasy, and romance. He has released poetry books, novellas, and recently released his first novel in 2018. When not writing, C.L. Williams can be found performing his poems at a poetry reading, selling his books at conventions and festivals, or reading and sharing the works of other independent authors.

SOLD
Katie Jaarsveld

Intro

I am old now. I forget how old, and I am not certain I ever really knew.

I will tell you what I do remember of my life as a tiny woman.

Sideshow

Chapter 1 First Experience

I never grew up, literally. My body only changed shape. My hair grew long. And my parents were paid money when people wanted to watch me perform. I loved to sing. It was the one thing that made me feel bigger than my life. If I was being stared at, my parents would charge for it.

One day the carnival came to town. They paraded down the street, performing while they walked.

There was a huge banner being carried by two of the tallest people I have ever seen. Announcing **The Greatest Carnival Alive**

They were followed by a man with a monkey sitting on a music box. The monkey would stand and dance around, he looked to be laughing at everyone. There were clowns on bicycles riding in circles and figure of eights. They looked like they would crash sometimes, but they never did. The clowns were short but not as short as me.

Then came a truck pulling cages with animals inside, it looked like a train of animals. I saw a gorilla in one, then a tiger at least it sounded like a big cat, I wasn't certain. The last animal I saw was a bear. The cage had a sign saying he performed tricks. I was so excited to see that.

There was a man walking around yelling, "Popcorn, peanuts, get your peanuts," in a loud, raspy voice. The smell of salty butter from the popcorn made me hungry. A girl was carrying cotton candy in a tray. There was even a girl selling cigarettes, stacked in neat rows, in a tray. Could you imagine? I'd never heard of such a thing.

Next in line were horses and women in dazzling costumes standing on their backs. One waved at me. She was so pretty. Following the ladies was a man riding on an elephant, sitting just behind her ears.

The man hit the elephant with a long stick which had a metal V-shaped tip on the end with one being straight and one curved out. The man made her get down on her knees. That made me so mad. The elephant was carrying him, and he hit her and made her bow. The nerve. I hadn't been that mad since someone tried to carry me like a doll. I yelled, but of course, no one heard me over the parade.

I stood on my stage in the front yard, (which was a box with stairs my father built from pallets) and watched them walk by.

There was music which sounded as if it was from a piano, but it had a metal tinging sound.

Next was a small truck with a banner on the side which said,

HUMAN CURIOSITIES

There came trailers and caravans with people walking alongside them, trying not to step in what the animals had left behind. The trailers were painted with the faces of the trailers' inhabitants. The Bearded Lady, Siamese Twins, Elephant Man, the Fat Lady, The Giant Twins, Dwarfs, Midget Clowns and many more.

I was intrigued. They were fantastic. Some of them looked above my head as if they didn't see me.

When the last caravan had gone by, they looked over to me. A man with tattoos all over himself blew me a kiss. When I looked around and saw no one near me, I winked back, and he smiled. The Bearded Lady waved, and I waved back. They were all being nice, well, the ones who saw me, at least.

A dwarf and midgets were handing out flyers. A dwarf ran up to me, handing me one, making sure I had a firm grip on it, then he backed away. He bowed to me. I smiled and curtseyed back to him. He laughed, waved and ran off.

Sideshow

I looked at the flyer. Attached was a free ticket for opening night. Tonight. I waved back so hard my box shook.

The flyer stated we would be greeted by the monkey on his music box, a fire-eater, the sword swallower, and someone selling popcorn as well as games to win balloons or toy animal prizes.

There would be bands made up of different races and oddities, dancers from different cultures performing to attract people to the main tent.

You could see the freaks for free with my ticket, and the animals. I couldn't stand still.

I was so excited I almost tripped running in the house. My parents were fighting. I listened. It wasn't hard with them yelling.

"What are we supposed to do with no extra money coming in?"

"Why are you yelling at me? You're the one who purchases lavish clothes to show her off in."

"Well, what do you want me to do, sell her to the circus?

I ran back outside and hid. Were my parents talking about selling me? I was their child. How could you sell your child? I wanted to run away and join myself. I had an even better idea. I would set it up to be rid of them if that was how they felt.

Joining the carnival would be perfect. I looked at the flyer and the free ticket attached.

Chapter 2 Sold

I waited until the house was quiet to go in. I wasn't sure they knew I was outside. They didn't like my being outside alone. My mom was sitting having a drink at the kitchen table. A drink and a cigarette were her choices after an argument she had won. I pondered over the results.

I simply stood there with the flyer in my hands. She saw the flyer and said nothing, so I handed it to her.

She looked at the flyer for some time while she finished her drink. Fingering the ticket, she didn't say a word. I hadn't seen this particular expression on her face before. She finally stopped and looked at me.

"I suppose you would like to go? There is a free ticket after all." She said it almost as a sneer. I was becoming scared. Mom didn't act that way toward me. Ever. She might have gotten irritated with me sometimes, but I tried to be good.

I didn't want to lose the chance to go, but I wasn't sure if I was supposed to say something or not. So, I just stood there wringing my hands.

She told me to go to my room until supper and she would talk with Father about it. I did as I was told, hoping it meant we could all go to the Carnival. The ticket was only good for opening night, and for one person.

I could hear their raised voices, but they weren't fighting. I was hoping that was a good thing. I was called to supper right after. Mom announced she and I would be going to the Carnival on opening night that night to use the free ticket.

I looked over to my Father. If I didn't know better, I'd say he looked sad while Mom looked more happy about going than I felt. My skin felt cold with goosebumps.

Sideshow

When she announced we might go to see a friend of hers, I suspected something was wrong. She never took me to see her friends as I was a distraction. Then she told me to wear my long, oriental dress with the slits and leggings, and she would be in to help me pack an overnight case, I knew something was definitely going on.

Father wouldn't look at me. He even got up from the table before he finished his supper, and it was our favorite dinner. He loved pot roast with gravy, potatoes, and carrots.

I took another bite, but I couldn't swallow it. When she went to refill her drink, I spat it out in my napkin. She came back, and I asked to be excused. She said we might be gone longer than a day and we could go out to someplace nice, so I needed to pack most of my clothes to have choices. I nodded and ran to my room.

I didn't want her to hear me crying. It would spoil the night at the Carnival. I walked around the house and I couldn't find my Father. So, I went back to my room and started pulling clothes out of drawers.

I decided to pack my favorite things. Somehow, I knew inside that I would never see my room again. I packed what I liked, including the shoes and make-up, most of which belonged to her. She wouldn't have approved but I also packed my favorite book and my comfortable clothes like leggings with long shirts, boots, and sundresses.

I liked the bright blue and sparkly light purple costumes with matching shoes. Pale pink lipstick. My beautiful red, oriental dress, and slippers. The perk of being tiny meant I could pack more.

I was leaving behind the gaudy, beaded costumes. The pink dress I hated, and the red lipstick.

I was doing this for me. I couldn't believe how stupid she thought I was that I didn't know what was happening.

I may have had a small body, but my brain was full sized.

Taking one last look at my room, I was satisfied I had everything I wanted to keep. I dragged my suitcase to the living room. Mother had her summer coat out and her handbag. I noticed she didn't even have her cosmetic bag with her. She wouldn't be gone long without it.

I walked around the house, making sure I wasn't forgetting anything I would miss. I wasn't.

For the first time, I noticed on the mantle there was one family picture of Mother and Father. None of me or the whole family. I thought there would have been. I wondered why I'd never noticed that before. Probably due to my height. I only saw it now because I was looking for it.

I went to the hall wardrobe and opened my suitcase. I pulled out my winter things and packed them. Mom gave me an odd look but said nothing. When I was satisfied I had everything from this house, I started to close my suitcase for the last time.

Father stopped me and put something in my suitcase, then fastened it closed. He patted me on the head and said, "Have a good life." Not a good time.

Sideshow

Chapter 3 Adjusting

I caught his hand in mine and hugged it. He looked at me with red eyes. Had he been crying? He coughed and took his hand away. Father smelled of alcohol. He said nothing when he left the room.

Mom announced it was time to go to the Carnival. I grabbed my backpack, which was from a doll, and put it on. I had seen my Father with it earlier, but I didn't say anything. It was time to go. I grabbed my suitcase and the flyer with my ticket. I was surprised when Mom offered to carry my case. She placed it in the back seat with me, not in the trunk. She didn't use the backseat, always saying, 'People with class only carry people in their seat. Everything else should be placed in the trunk.'

I tried not to cry. I wouldn't give her that satisfaction. We pulled away from our home and I waved goodbye.

In my mind, I was plotting how to get even with my Mother and her perfectly made-up face, dyed hair, and manicured nails. Maybe if she didn't look so perfect, I mused. My Father just letting her take me away was just as unforgivable, red eyes, tears or not.

We arrived at the carnival right on time on opening night. They were just starting to allow admissions.

I was standing, looking out the window of the car, trying to see. Mother braked hard, making my head bump on the window. Looking in the rearview mirror, she had a smile on her face as I rubbed my sore head.

When we got out, she took my suitcase. I didn't say anything. She didn't hold my hand or carry me, but she didn't usually anyway.

There was a monkey sitting on his music box with a man cranking the handle by the window where they took my ticket and Mother purchased hers. She gave me a frown.

There was a sword swallower and a Fire-breather was after that. They were amazing. The snake charmer lady was beautiful but scary. The snake was huge and wrapped itself around her. She acted like she was going to kiss it. I read in my stories where you kissed a frog to get a prince, not a snake. I wanted to remind her, but I looked the other way. I could hear her laughing and it was a pretty sound.

I smelled the salted butter popcorn, but I didn't dare to ask for any, even though I was hungry.

Before the big top tent were performers dancing and speaking in languages I had never heard.

I saw the sign for the Human Curiosities and wanted to go there. She saw me looking and had the same sinister smile again. She suggested we go that way. A man in a black tuxedo stood and walked toward us. He introduced himself as the owner and Ringmaster. He had been talking with other people, whom he dismissed, leaving the patio table and chairs unoccupied.

He was looking mostly at me but shook Mother's hand. You could tell it irritated her since she wanted the attention. He asked if he could help me onto the table, so we could speak face to face. I nodded, and he sat me in the middle of the table, nodding for Mother to sit. He had several questions such as my height, my age, then looked at Mother and asked about my birth certificate, shot record, and medical information. His curled mustache twitched when he spoke, and I tried not to laugh. I didn't want to appear rude.

I answered the first question. "47cm," I replied with a smile. He smiled back with a kindness. I knew my height from the doctor's office. She answered, "She's 18," with regards to my age. He was shaking his head no. She handed the man some papers in a big envelope. He pulled the important looking papers out of the envelope and read them.

He looked from the papers to me. Shaking his head, he beckoned to someone to come out of the trailer.

A very tall lady stepped out from the open door of the nearest trailer and handed Mom some papers to sign, which were signed by the man too, then stamped by the tall lady in the dress suit. She had a pretty smile.

After the papers were signed, he handed Mother a thick brown envelope tied with a string. She pulled at the string to open it and cut her finger. No one said a word.

Everyone stood, and I wondered what I missed. I should have been paying attention not daydreaming, but the big words like *'guardianship and legal custody'* were confusing. The lady carried my suitcase to the trailer and came back out. She saw me look toward it and assured me it was safe there. She smiled and asked if she could carry me if I would show her how. She had a deep voice, deeper than my Father's. Her hands were bigger than his.

I said to hold me like a toddler sitting up. She got it right the first time. It was very comfortable. I could see so much because she was so tall.

My Mother held out her hand to shake with the Ringmaster. He didn't take her hand and pointed to the blood dripping from her finger. She took a handkerchief from her purse and wrapped it around her finger.

Mother walked off without looking back. She didn't even tell me goodbye. That was the day I was sold to the Carnival.

"You know what's happening don't you, little one?" I shook my head yes. "I'm Mia," was all I could say. I was trying hard not to cry, but I really wanted someone to hold me while I cried.

Sideshow

Chapter 4 Fitting In With Other Freaks

Samantha thought I needed my first night to adjust and said she would explain things tomorrow and introduce me to everyone then.

We had corn dogs for dinner and relaxed on the patio. We could hear all the noise and excitement, but I was happy for some peace and time to adjust.

Samantha said she needed to do something and came back with popcorn. I was so excited and ate most or a lot of the popcorn by myself. She teased that I ate my weight in popcorn. I wasn't sure what it meant but we both laughed about it.

She explained to me that being 'sold' didn't mean exactly that. I would earn cash wages to save because I was now an employee and could come and go at a later date if I chose, once my 'sold contract' was up. I also had to be of legal age, (whatever that meant). This was one of the good Carnivals to work for and she had been there for lots of years.

If it was okay with me, I would be living with Samantha. I was very happy to hear that. So happy that I jumped up from sitting on the table and hugged her. I think she had a tear. I know I did, but for happiness. Someone wanted me.

I would sleep in Samantha's trailer on a bed which looked made for me. It was off to the side so Samantha wouldn't step on it. She did have kind of big feet. I teased her she could use my bed for a shoe if she had another bed. She thought it was funny.

My bed had a beautiful silk blanket with matching pillows. Samantha had made them from some of her scarves for me.

My clothes were partially unpacked in a wardrobe which suited my height. I could get my own clothes out without a stool or help. It felt good.

I looked in my suitcase to finish unpacking and to see what my Father had put in there. It was a photo of me as a baby. That was all. I went to my backpack to see what my Father had placed in there. A tube of red lipstick.

He knew I hated red lips. I would never wear it again, it reminded me of her. Or maybe I should wear it. To remind me of what I needed to do to her. Maybe. I was so mad I was shaking.

Samantha was talking to me, but I didn't hear her. I went back to my suitcase. Samantha was staring at me with her mouth open when I turned around. I had been squeezing my fists so tight they dripped blood.

"Oh no, child, NO! You can't let them do that to you." She had picked me up and was carrying me, telling me to shush. I tried to pull back and she held me tighter, til I started to cry. Then I cried and it all came forward. All of my mother's emotional abuse and jealousy, her being hateful to my father. My father not fighting for me.

I cried until I was almost asleep. Samantha rocked me and held me like a child who was loved and cherished. I gave her a hug and she hugged back.

She sat me on her chair and came back with a warm washcloth and a tube of ointment. Saying thank you, I washed my face. I didn't have much makeup on, so it didn't take long to remove it. Looking at my blood on Samantha's beautiful clothes, I apologized. "What, this old thing?" She brushed at the blood as if to make it disappear. She winked then helped me clean the blood off my hands. It was already dry, but she put ointment on the small cuts anyway.

Sideshow

I jumped down from her chair and asked Samantha where the small furniture came from. She said one of the dwarfs was a craftsman in woodworking. I asked to meet him, so I could give him my thanks.

Samantha threw on a shawl, then took me to meet this dwarf. He was working in a tent/workshop. It had a wooden wall at the back with a door, but the front and sides were canvas material with the front, twin door flaps tied open.

He was the same one who had given me my ticket to the Carnival. She introduced us. "Derek, I would like you to meet Mia." He stopped what he was working on and looked around. Upon seeing me he bowed, and I replied with a curtsey. When we started laughing, Samantha looked confused, so Derek filled her in.

"So, you see, little one, you know two people here now." Samantha pointed out.

Derek came over and shook my hand as I was thanking him for my bed and wardrobe. My hand felt all tingly. He smiled at me. I think he felt it too.

He was working without a shirt on. He looked like a small, black bodybuilder with ice blue eyes. He slipped a tank on. I wished he would leave it off. He was very cute. Samantha chose that time to whisper, "He's single." I elbowed her somewhere, not taking my eyes off him. I heard her chuckle.

I knew I was blushing, and I suspected Derek saw and heard everything because his cheeks were a little red too. With the smile on his face beaming, I'm fairly certain he was happy.

Sideshow

Chapter 5 Preparations

Just after our blush encounter, we heard someone yelling his name. I guess he'd lost track of time. Since it was opening night, he needed to get ready for his stunts in the big tent. He covered whatever he was working on and started to run out of his tent.

He ran back and kissed my cheek, then ran back out, waving and yelling that he'd see us later.

I was in an excited shock. My first kiss, if a kiss on the cheek counted. To me it did. Samantha was laughing and had her hands clasped together.

We walked back toward Samantha's wagon and decided against it. Instead, we went to the 'mess hall'. Samantha explained it was an open tent in the middle of where our wagons were, away from the public. It was where Shorty and his giant wife, Matilda made and served our meals, as well as a place to visit, relax, have meetings, basically our communication center.

She introduced me to Shorty and Matilda, as well as several who didn't work on opening night during the show or were on breaks. Sometimes the other Carnival workers stopped by, but mostly this was the 'Freak Zone'.

After we had a cola and visited for a bit, I started yawning. Samantha saw, and we excused ourselves, saying it had been a long day. They acted like they understood. They both gave me a hug and welcomed me.

Samantha gave them both a hug. She offered to carry me, but I declined, wanting to learn my way around from my view.

We were almost to our wagon when we saw people coming and going. Opening night was at a close. Now was the time for the others to tend to the animals and clean the tent. Then everyone would settle in for the night. Everyone helped with chores except the performers. They only cleaned their own trailers or hired someone who did, since the Ringmaster tolerated no slobs in this Carnival.

We saw the Ringmaster near our wagon. He waved and walked toward us. "I've been looking for you two." He smiled and asked how my fitting in was going. Samantha smiled and said she thought it was fine. I smiled and told him I was being treated with kindness and liked the people I'd met so far.

"Anytime you need to talk, my trailer is at the end of the path, by the patio table. It's the line between the performers and the freaks." He didn't say the terms in disgust or anything bad. I liked that.

"Tomorrow we will talk with Derek, the craftsman, and ask him to build your doll box. You will be put on display as 'A living doll," if you don't mind. Samantha will help you with costumes, alterations, or anything you need done. She is a seamstress with strong talents and imagination. Oh, there's Derek now."

The Ringmaster waved Derek over. He was smiling at us. He bowed, and I curtseyed. The Ringmaster looked between us curiously but said nothing. Samantha coughed but I could hear the laughter she was trying to mask.

"I guess you two know each other. Derek, I will need you to build an intricate box for 'Our living doll'. Derek was blushing.

Samantha took the Ringmaster to the side and something in low tones. I heard, 'budding romance' in the whispering. I hoped they were right.

Derek said after breakfast we could get started. If we would meet him at his workshop. I agreed. Samantha and the Ringmaster joined us again.

Sideshow

We told of the plan to start after breakfast. Samantha was good with the plan and the Ringmaster agreed. Derek stated he would sketch it up tonight before sleeping.

Derek gave me another kiss on the cheek. Samantha gave a wave and the Ringmaster only said goodnight.

Samantha didn't hold back the laughter this time as we watched Derek and the Ringmaster walk away. Derek was looking back, waving.

"Come on little one, looks like you have a busy day tomorrow, Mia." She touched the top of my head. It reminded me of Father. I wondered how he was doing and if he missed me.

At our wagon, I dressed for bed while Samantha was in the bathroom getting ready for bed. She was talking to me, but I was thinking of Derek and not paying attention. I heard the, *I look different without makeup*. I didn't care. She's Samantha.

I had just sat down on my bed when she walked out of the bathroom, not looking like Samantha. I closed my mouth as soon as I realized it was open.

Samantha was talking and with my eyes closed, I could tell it was her. The room smelled of her vanilla perfume. I opened my eyes and Samantha had her back to me. Her hair hung in a long blonde braid. When she turned around she looked more like a male.

I knew I was staring, with my head tilted to the side. She knelt down by me and held out her hands. They were Samantha's hands. "Do you know who I am?" The question held a sadness to it. I smiled and laid my hands in hers. "You're my best friend, Samantha." One tear was sliding down her face. I added, "with scruff." She let out a laugh. Soon we were both laughing hard. It felt good.

Sideshow

The woman used to be Sam and was now Samantha. She was very kind to me and my best friend, if not family.

Across the compound, a dwarf heard our laughter and slept the best he had slept in a long time.

Chapter 6 Showcased As A Living Doll

I slept well but I couldn't get dressed fast enough. I would be spending time with Derek today. I planned to get to know him very well.

Samantha would show me the way, but she had duties to perform today. She was certain Derek would take good care of me, she kept assuring me I would be in good hands. I knew she was teasing me.

The Carnival people were very busy today. Some were practicing or cleaning. Some were having breakfast. We stopped and ate pancakes with Shorty. His wife made the best coffee I had ever tasted.

After breakfast, Samantha stopped in front of Derek's and winked, waving goodbye.

Derek was sitting on an engraved bench having coffee. When he saw me, he stood and walked over. He offered to show me around his shop.

The workshop was grand. Tools I had never seen before hung on a pegboard. The was a wall with sketches and measurements. A long workbench held projects in varying stages of being completed. He looked like he was building many things.

I kept looking at his tools. I had a score to settle and I was planning it out carefully. Derek saw me looking his tools over. He may have known what I was thinking. I wondered if he ever had those thoughts, but I didn't know how he came to be at the Carnival.

One of the sketches was of a house. At the back of the workshop was a house. He had built his own house on wheels. Each room was customized to his height. It was beautiful. That explained why the back of his workshop had a wooden wall and a door.

Sideshow

I was going to ask if I could see it. He came over and took my hand, leading me out of the workshop as a bell rang. He said it was time for lunch.

I was introduced to many freaks of all shapes and sizes. I was the smallest. Some of them were a little standoffish at first. Not knowing what to make of me or my height. I supposed a few were afraid they could hurt me. To be honest, the thought had occurred to me as well.

Samantha was there for lunch. She usually liked to carry me around, so I wouldn't get stepped on. However, Derek presented me with a platform-type stroller. He lifted me to sit on it. It was a throne and I could be wheeled around by him because it looked like he'd made the height for that very reason. I liked the idea of us spending time alone together.

It was made from stroller wheels and a frame, but the baby bucket was gone and there was a grand, engraved chair made to fit in the frame. The chair could be used separately as well. There was even a soft pillow, I suspected Samantha had made that. It was the most beautiful thing I had ever seen.

I kissed him on the mouth in front of everyone. While some clapped and cheered, others simply shook their heads and smiled.

The Ringmaster sat down with us. He showed me a flyer headlining me with the freaks as a Living Doll. I would go on display that night. I frowned at being new and headlined. I didn't want it to create animosity between myself and the other freaks.

Samantha explained all freaks were headlined at least once, especially new members, once everyone was sure they would fit in with the family. I felt better with the knowledge that all freaks were given their moment. Even better, now that I had a real family.

Sometimes I would sit on my new chair, (so the Ringmaster knew about it). Other times I would be 'standing', but actually, would be sitting on a stool, which my dress would cover. In a glass case with a hidden hinge on the inside so I could get out if I wanted to, so I wouldn't get scared. All I had to do was wave to people and smile.

I liked the box because people couldn't touch me or poke me to make sure I was real. When I was on my chair, I would sit and eat popcorn while they stared at me. It was great fun for the people and for me. I looked at it like we were being amusement for each other.

I saw my face on a newspaper with Samantha. It said she was my mom and we both had a laugh at it. So, did Derek and most of the freaks.

Reporters hadn't taken photos, so I was surprised to see our picture.

One quiet night, I was sitting on my stool in my box, waiting for Samantha to come and get me, which was our routine at the end of the night. It was almost close when a man walked into the tent. I sat still and watched him. I couldn't see his face, but I felt something. There was something familiar about him, the way he stood and walked.

Father. It was my father.

He came up and looked at me with my new clothes. My chair sitting beside my box.

"I should have asked for more money for you." His voice was dripping with hatred.

Why? I thought, feeling a panic form in my chest. They sold me. They didn't get to talk to me that way.

Sideshow

He picked up my chair and repeatedly hit it against the wooden frame of my box. It made the glass I was enclosed in vibrate and shatter, showering me with the glass and wood splinters from the box frame. The box Derek had made for me.

I was so scared I started to cry—then something switched, and I became mad. So mad I couldn't stand still. I opened the hidden hinge on the inside of my box and stepped out. I pulled the long crochet hook out of my shawl I was making and stabbed him in the eye so hard that the hook on the end pulled his eye right out of the socket.

He was screaming and writhing on the ground in pain. Samantha came running in at that time. I didn't say anything except, "My father" and shook his eye on the hook.

Derek walked in and assessed the area after hearing someone wail. He saw me with an eyeball, my box broken, chair damaged, then looked at the man.

"Dad?" was the one only question. He sounded amused. Derek went and tied the tent closed. It was almost time to close for the night anyway. "What do we do now?" Samantha inquired with a smile. Father had passed out. He never could stand pain.

Chapter 7 Clean Up

News spread quickly among the freaks about what had happened to me. Shorty came with a butcher's ax, Matilda had a sewing kit, Samantha picked up garden scissors from somewhere. Derek had a power tool I hadn't seen before. Someone took the pinned eyeball from my hand.

At one time I had a father. What had attacked me? I had no idea what he was.

The Ringmaster came and took me to his trailer. There was a woman there, who I knew as the Bearded Lady. He sat me on the table and she began removing hairpins and glass, then glass with splinters from my hair and clothes. Luckily, I only had a few scratches, nothing deep.

I heard someone scream and I jumped. The Bearded Lady said, "Newcomer" in a monotone voice. Like that was supposed to answer all questions. She continued cleaning glass slivers off me without stopping.

After I was all clean, the Ringmaster carried me to my wagon, asking for the clothes I had on, at the doorway. He pulled the door almost closed and I handed them to him, where he shook them out.

I changed into a long t-shirt and leggings with slippers. He asked for my brush, so he could brush out any remaining debris. I was surprised he asked, still, I got my brush for him. My damaged but not broken, chair was there on its stand. He sat me on my chair while he brushed my hair.

He was very methodical, and I was sure he had removed all the debris. I would still be careful when I washed it, just to be on the safe side.

Sideshow

When Samantha returned to the tent, the Ringmaster left. I thanked him, but he kept walking. Samantha didn't talk either.

Why was no one talking to me? I didn't do anything wrong. I thought about looking for Derek, but I wouldn't be able to handle him not talking with me. Maybe I could go to the mess hall? The Ringmaster said if I ever needed him, to go to his trailer.

I ran to his trailer and knocked but no one answered. I decided to wait by the patio. I sat on a brick near a chair with my back to the tree.

I heard the Ringmaster and a man talking about the Newcomers. There would be two of them, to begin with. A man and a woman. More would be joining. They would be short term with the Carnival. He wasn't sure they would survive to move to the next town with us.

Survive? I was not really sure what that meant, and eavesdropping wasn't a good thing to practice.

I coughed so they would know I was there. The Ringmaster looked around and I stood up, not that it helped. When he saw me, he looked something between sad and worn out.

"Come on Mia, let's go inside the trailer to talk." He said in a resigned voice. Looking at the man he was talking to he said, "Better get Samantha for this, Grady." The man nodded and left.

The Ringmaster poured a couple of drinks. He looked around for something and looked triumphant when he found a beautiful ceramic thimble. He poured some of the same drink into it and handed it to me. He took a large drink from one of the glasses he poured then filled it back up.

Sideshow

I took a big drink too and coughed. My eyes burned, and I couldn't breathe. He looked at me as if to ask if I was alright. I shook my head yes, took a deep breath, coughed and took another drink. It was easier this time. He smiled and filled my thimble.

I had a feeling I was going to know what a hangover was tomorrow.

Samantha didn't knock on arrival, she just walked in. Only to see the Ringmaster and I filling our glasses, or thimbles a third time. She reached over like she was going to take my thimble and I shook my head no. She drew her hand back and sat down.

She pointed to the third glass and we shook our heads yes. She downed it in one swallow, followed by a wheeze and a cough. "Fill 'er up." He filled her glass for a second round. All I could think was that if I got drunk, anyone could carry me home. If Samantha was drunk, it would take all the freaks to help her stumble home. It made me laugh.

Grady came back and announced they were moving my 'display'. The Ringmaster gave a thumbs up and downed his drink, leaving with Grady.

Samantha downed her drink, so I finished mine too. I was ready for bed. Samantha bent down to scoop me up and I jumped back, nearly tripping over my own feet. We both laughed. It was going to be interesting to see how we made it back to the wagon.

Fortunately, someone almost as tall as Samantha showed up. Andy, I think his name was. I was hoping to see Derek but a clown whose name or face I didn't get because my head felt swollen, helped me back to the wagon.

Sideshow

Chapter 8 Questions and Answers or Not

I woke to someone pounding on the door. Shorty. He had a thermos of coffee, eggs, bacon, sausage, and toast. He said he'd slaughtered a pig to get rid of my hangover. He winked and smiled. The smell of coffee woke Samantha. She wasn't all in bed, half of her was hanging off. I used a feather boa on her feet to wake her.

Apparently, all that did was make her need to pee, the way she jumped up and hit her head. I was laughing so hard I almost spat my food out.

When she re-appeared, she said we had a meeting with the Ringmaster first thing that morning. After breakfast and most of all, coffee.

While I didn't care for the sound of that, I finished my breakfast and some of hers. I'd never eaten that much. It must have been alcohol induced.

We took turns in the shower and dressed for the meeting. It was at the mess hall, so it involved everyone.

Samantha grabbed our tray and we walked over to the mess hall, handing it over to Matilda. She looked happy we ate. We were the last two to arrive, I guessed. Derek wasn't there yet but the Ringmaster was starting.

"I'll start off with the unpleasantness which occurred last evening." I felt like I was going to lose my breakfast as the memories flooded in.

The Ringmaster looked at me. He looked apologetic. I nodded for him to continue. He cleared his throat.

"Mia was attacked last night. The identity of the man makes no difference. Mia did well defend herself in removing his eye, incapacitating her attacker until help arrived. Thank you, Samantha." Samantha nodded with tears in her eyes.

"Mia hasn't been with us long enough to know all the rules, or even to be familiar with how this family is." He looked right at me and I could hear the emotion in his voice.

"This family will defend each other to the death. Literally. Even if it means the death of someone who threatens us.

"The man who attacked you will be staying with the Carnival for a couple of days." I took a deep breath and started to speak.

"Shush and listen now." His voice held a harsh, hard tone. "He was dealt with. You removed an eye. Samantha removed the other one with gardening shears. His eyes have been sewn shut by Samantha. His tongue was cut out by Derek and sewn by Matilda. The man cannot speak against you, or any of us. Matilda will care for him until CHP remove him."

I had my hand over my mouth. I was in shock and hearing the horrifying story, I pictured a stranger. The man last night was not my father.

"I called in Carnival Horror Performers to finish this show with us. They are clowns, of sorts. What they really are, is a clean-up crew. They also do damage control, so there is no bad publicity or any mention of the man ever being here, or what was done with him. He will cease to exist."

"There is one thing all of you should know. The CHP as they prefer to be called, do not work for money or favors. They require a pound of flesh. They removed it from this man in the early hours this morning, by removing his limbs. He signed papers with blood, indicating he had joined us of his own free will. He has no name and will be referred to as *It,* as well as the others, for the duration of their stay."

I saw others staring toward the path to the regular performers. A Fire-breather was walking toward us. Everyone sat still.

The Ringmaster continued, "This is Monroe, the Fire-breather. He seared the wounds closed on the injured man after the CHP were finished dealing with him."

He walked up to me. "I am Monroe and it was my honor to defend you." He nodded and walked away.

I didn't know what to say. I was overwhelmed, mad that this had to happen, and happy that I had others who wanted me there, who would do anything to protect me. But I needed to get away. I jumped down and ran.

No one said anything, they just let me go. I ran until I was out of breath. Realistically, it probably wasn't far, but it was space and I needed the air.

Chapter 9 Invitations

I sat for what seemed just a short while, I'm guessing it was much longer since I heard the bell, announcing meal time.

I pondered over the fact, a man was sitting somewhere without eyes, a tongue, no limbs. I didn't feel sorry for him, he was being cared for until whatever was decided for him. Either way, it had nothing to do with me.

As far as I knew, my real father, not this thing that showed up last night, was living his every day, dull life, being bullied by Mother. My mind had to stay in that place. Mother would get hers too.

I stood and walked back to the wagon. I wanted sleep. I took the long way around to avoid running into anyone. There were no tents, only tall (for me) grass. I reached my wagon unnoticed and went to sleep.

Surprisingly, I guess I passed out. Someone was banging on the wagon door. It was Grady. He said Matilda wanted to see me. I looked for my slippers until he pointed at my feet. I had fallen asleep with them on.

Matilda was cleaning up from dinner. I had missed two meals today. "Come, child, eat. It's only pulled pork BBQ, but we are cleaning up the pig we slaughtered. Tomorrow will be bacon, ham and whatever else we use." Matilda had a swing to her step and reminded me of what a grandmother would be like if I had ever had one.

I picked at my food, not really hungry. Matilda was frowning at me. "Pushing it around your plate won't do you any good. You need to eat, child." I set the fork down and pushed the plate away.

"I'm sorry. The thought of eating meat and knowing a man lost his limbs…" My voice trailed off and I bowed my head. I knew she wouldn't feed us body parts. I just couldn't swallow, really anything right now.

"Child, that's pure meat. I understand the weak stomach though." She sighed and asked if I wanted anything else.

"Fried toast and your wild blueberry jelly?" I asked sheepishly. Matilda gave a big grin and turned on the fire to make my fried toast.

I always liked the butter cooked into the toast. The smell of the butter cooking made my stomach growl. The toaster made even the best bread taste of cardboard, no matter what you slathered on it.

While I was eating my toast and jelly, Matilda poured me a glass of milk bigger than I was. "I have homemade peanut butter for your pancakes tomorrow too". She winked at me. I have no idea how she knew I liked peanut butter on pancakes.

After I finished eating, Matilda confessed why she had me sent for. "I know all about that man and what he said to you, what he did to your things. You were right about what you did. He told everything before we cut his tongue out. My eyes started to water. Matilda handed me a handkerchief. It smelled like butter and cake.

"Child, just you forget all about it. We know about her too. His wife. She was no Mother to you, Mia. She'll be getting hers too." I could only hope.

Matilda handed me a piece of paper. It was a flyer to attend the Carnival and Freakshow. One night only.

"Some certain families are getting an invite to the Carnival. They are bad people, like the one who tried to hurt you last night. He was carrying a money demand. He was wanting more money for you, from when they sold you." She sighed and continued on.

Sideshow

"We are going to have a few disfigured freaks for a few days, then them CHP boys will clean up." She had her voice down low like she didn't want anyone to hear what she was telling me.

The more I heard, the madder I became. "How can I help?" Matilda grinned and handed me an envelope for Mother's address. I addressed it and she put it in her apron pocket. It looked like she had collected a few envelopes.

"How many will be attending the *special invitation*?" I wasn't sure why I was whispering. I would think everyone knew what would happen.

"We have one more night open to the public, tonight. The next night will be special. It will be the night before we pack up and roll out. That gives us a day and we don't look like we know anything, since we're not in a hurry. There will be three people attending, at the least. You know one, another for Samantha, and the other will be for Derek. You don't know it, but you all are from around the same area."

Sideshow

Chapter 10 Plan

The invitations were hand delivered that evening by Monroe. He was handsome and would make Mother feel special. I didn't know about the others who were invited, but I was guessing they were a parent or caregiver too.

Monroe came to the mess hall to let us know all the letters were delivered and accepted. All three would be attending for their special showing. I was sitting on my chair and asked him for a hug. He smiled and hugged me back. Monroe walked back down the path, whistling.

I sat back down, contemplating the upcoming deeds. I knew Sam needed closure from her past. I hadn't seen Derek and I missed him. I didn't know if he was okay or okay with what was going to happen.

Derek chose that time to make an appearance. It was only Shorty, Matilda and me there. They disappeared. Derek and I just stared at each other. He came over to my chair and hugged me. I held him as long as he let me. We exchanged a kiss that made someone watching, whistle. A grin broke us apart. "Voyeur," Derek yelled into the shadows.

It was Samantha *and* the Ringmaster. "A fella can't get no privacy around here." He grumbled but smiled too.

Shorty and Matilda reappeared too, all smiles.

The Ringmaster invited us all to sit down. Derek set me back on my chair and sat next to me, still holding my hand.

"Our family of freaks here, and a few performers, along with CHP will be changed after tomorrow night. Everyone is in agreement as to what needs to be done. In the past, we have eliminated threats, eliminated the ones who hurt or would hurt our family here. Also, the CHP will not be allowed in the Freak camp area, unless it is to remove a threat." The Ringmaster sounded stern and looked tired.

"I suggest you all get a good night's rest tonight. Tomorrow will be exhausting. In the meantime, I need to go finish tonight's final performance before we close out." The Ringmaster stood, dusted imaginary dust from his tux and stood tall, walking back to the big tent.

Matilda brought a fresh pot of coffee from the campfire and some apple pie, fresh from the stone oven. I really wasn't hungry, but it smelled too good to resist. I loved the smell of cinnamon and butter.

We ate in silence, each of us contemplating what we needed to do in order to have closure and move on to happy lives.

After we helped Matilda clean the mess hall, we all said our goodnights and went our separate ways. Except for Derek, who pushed my chair and saw Samantha and I to our wagon. Samantha said goodnight and went in. Derek and I exchanged a kiss and just held each other for a moment. He lifted me down and helped me into the wagon, calling goodnight to Samantha. I gave one more kiss before closing the door.

Derek was singing as he walked away.

The next morning was brought to us with a commotion. Matilda was ringing the bell hard, which meant trouble. "The CHP are in our camp," she was screaming her vast lungs out. Matilda was having a fit! Before breakfast! The Ringmaster had firmly stated they would not be allowed in the Freak camp.

We jumped up and got dressed. We heard yelling, and I'm positive she had been throwing pans and everything else at them.

Sideshow

I heard the Ringmaster yell, and everyone was silent. The Fire-breather, Monroe came up behind him, trying to tell him something.

Samantha and I reached the mess hall right behind the Ringmaster and Monroe. "The *It* died during the night, lasting two days. His real name was not recorded, for we did not know it. We had him for the shortest duration. The CHP have disposed of the body, feeding it to the pigs. Any bones or parts remaining will be ground into dust, into the ground, making a nice fertilizer. We always till up the ground where hogs have been, so there will be nothing suspicious. That is all which will be said on this matter."

The Ringmaster and Monroe sat and requested coffee. Some CHP had picked up her pans and Matilda pointed to the CHP to sit. I guessed everyone was having coffee this morning.

I should have felt remorse, but in fact, I only felt relief. Part of my nightmare had ended. A man I had called Father was non-existent. All that was left was a hateful, mean man. Maybe it's who he was all along.

I wouldn't torture myself with what-might-have-beens or what-ifs. It ended.

Tonight, Mother would get hers.

Chapter 11 Plan in Motion

Now to make a plan. First of all, I'd needed a big mirror. Since Mother was always perfectly made up, I thought it should be permanent. She wouldn't look good with wrinkles, for starters.

The skin on her face should be pulled tight. An alligator clamp on the sides of each ear. Better yet, she never wanted pierced ears because she felt the holes would disfigure her, so she wore clips. We could make a hole on the outside rim where the cartilage was, on each ear and pull them back with wires until they touched the back of her head. Secure them there with the wire.

A grinder on her cheeks would give her the rosy glow she was always trying for. She always told me beauty was pain. I'd be taking advice from her on that one.

Use blue paint for eyeshadow. It was her favorite color. We might need to thin it with turpentine, so it spreads smoothly.

Industrial glue for her eyelashes. We wouldn't want them to come off. I saw a can in Derek's shop.

Mother only said mean things, so we'd cut her tongue out, to give her inner beauty a chance to shine.

For her red lips, lipstick wouldn't be good enough. Sear them with a hot poker. That way she'd have the red, full lips she always wanted.

She was always breaking her nails, so maybe we should remove them for her.

She hated her underarm flab, and her fat thighs so, remove her arms and legs. She would be so much happier with all of her problem beauty areas fixed.

Sideshow

And to think, with all the mean things she had said to Father and myself, I'd be the one to make certain she'd be beautiful for the rest of her life.

The bell rang for meal time. Matilda had still made us a meal, in the midst of the commotion.

Samantha was nowhere to be seen.

I still had on my longish t-shirt, leggings, and flats. They would do for now. I was small, but my body was shaped like an adult. All of my limbs were in proportion to my body. I looked like a beautiful woman shrunk in size. However, there would be no make-up on this woman for today, and I brushed my long hair into a ponytail.

It was quiet, except for people eating and cutlery touching plates. Several were finished by the time I arrived at the mess area.

Matilda saw me and came over to help me into a tall chair with arms. To eat *at* the table instead of *on* it. I knew from the carvings, it was Derek's craftsmanship.

She walked away before I could ask when he brought it down. When did he have time? Samantha appeared and sat down beside me. She didn't look so well. Exhausted would be my guess. She gave me a tired smile and touched my hand.

"Derek finished it last night and asked me to bring it up." She gave me a half-hearted smile.

Matilda set homemade peanut butter and blueberry syrup on the table. A minute later, I had a stack of pancakes the size of half dollars. Just my size. I could smell the warm bananas. Yum.

I was so busy spreading peanut butter and eating, I didn't notice a glass of milk being set down by me, or Derek standing there, waiting for a hello.

"Remind me to never disturb you when you're eating."
Derek sounded like he was pouting, he looked it too.

Samantha let out a little laugh. "As if you could?!"

Derek leaned over, I thought for a kiss, but it was to
wipe peanut butter off the corner of my mouth.

"Hey! I was saving that for later." I tried to act
indignant.

"Not if you want a kiss from me, baby doll. I'm not into
peanut butter like you are." He stuck his tongue out at me
and I promptly wiped my fork with peanut butter on it, on
his tongue. He drew his tongue back in his mouth. "Hey,
that stuff's not bad."

Matilda came up behind him and lifted him onto a seat
beside me. "Good, then eat up, lover man." She sat on the
other side of him, chuckling.

We were all laughing and watching to see what his next
move would be. He took a spoon of peanut butter, placing
it on the plate by his pancakes. He cut a piece and wiped
up some peanut butter with it.

"Man, store-bought stuff has nothing on this," and
promptly cut another mouthful.

"That's what I thought." Matilda mused out loud.
Shorty brought over cups, along with the coffee pot. We
were the last to eat, I supposed.

The Ringmaster and Monroe were coming up the path.
I was beginning to think they only came around to deliver
bad news.

Shorty went to make more pancakes. Monroe saw what
we were eating. "Man, you guys eat well on this side of
camp."

Shorty yelled, "Breakfast will be done soon, so sit
down." You didn't have to tell the Fire-breather twice.

Chapter 12 Newcomers

After we all had eaten, we wanted a nap. Instead, the Ringmaster asked if we were ready to reveal our plans with CHP, so they would have their plans sorted out as well. I said I was ready. Monroe went to get the CHP.

Samantha and Derek were surprised I was ready. "I've thought on it all night." Was all I could say. They both shook their heads in agreement.

The head of CHP was a bit creepy, but nothing worse than what I was planning. He went by Sander and looked a bit of a badass, even with his clown face on. I pulled out the list of what needed to be done and in what order.

Sander looked me up and down, letting out a long whistle. "Remind me to never piss you off. But if you ever want to change professions, look me up." He winked. I saw steam come from both Derek and the Ringmaster. Sander noticed. "Just kidding guys, relax. It's serious enough." At that, we were all in agreement.

Samantha and Derek read over my list. "Mine is nowhere that detailed," Derek admitted. Samantha said, "Mine would just be slice and dice. An apology would be nice, but I'm not holding my breath for it, excuse the pun."

"Okay, Mia will deal with hers first. We'll get everything in there that she'll need, plus whoever will help with the different tasks. Let's get this done folks, so we can go to the ranch to recuperate."

The ranch was the Ringmasters ranch. Everyone who didn't have outside family was expected to stay at his ranch until the next scheduled booking. Freaks and performers alike.

I asked Samantha for her big mirror, a hollow piercing needle, large gauge. She went to get them for me.

Derek, I asked for pliers, wire, blue paint, thinned a little. I wouldn't need much. A grinder with harsh sandpaper on it, Industrial glue, heated metal of some kind and lastly, his bonesaw.

Matilda offered her garden shears and asked if she could have the honors. I was fine with that.

I had her red lipstick to outline where I would burn her.

I would see her in the clothes I had on, only because it would infuriate her. Plus, the bare minimum of makeup, my hair braided. Everything she hated. Oh, and I would be reading my book.

The stage was set, so I went and got ready. By the time I was back, everything I had requested was in the tent, with my chair on the table for her to view me.

Samantha, the Ringmaster, and Derek would be waiting behind the tent with Sander. Monroe would be escorting her through the tents. Matilda was on hand to cut her tongue as soon as it was needed.

Derek gave me a kiss and sat me on my chair, exiting through the tent flaps.

I took a deep breath as soon as I heard Monroe and Mother coming down the walkway which had public access. There was an old wooden chair not far from me. That must have been from the Ringmaster. I looked over at Samantha's mirror. I looked amazingly calm, with a little pissed mixed in for good measure.

As soon as Mother saw me, I saw hatred. I have no idea what she expected, but I guarantee, this night was not it.

She smelled sickeningly sweet of too much perfume. Her face and clothing were perfect, except that she had stepped in horse shit. Wonder how that happened. I really didn't want to be amused at the moment.

"Well, you're still here, Mia. I thought they would have the common sense to sell you off or do away with you. You look atrocious, where are the clothes we wasted money on? I suppose they needed a ragged looking doll." She sneered at me, the venom dripping from her mouth.

If the Firebreather had a shovel or heavy object, she would have stopped speaking.

"Your Father left, you know, almost a week ago now. He was never good for anything, never amounted to anything. Would never have been anything."

I couldn't help smiling. Once this started, she would never say a hateful word again.

Chapter 13 Punishment Round One

"Why would you have cause to smile, you little nothing?"

Matilda heard enough. She stood, and Mother yelled. "Sit back down you cow, this is between me and that, that—

Is as far as she got before Shorty hit her upside her head with a shovel. The sound of the dull thud made me jump. Matilda picked her up and dropped her in the chair, facing the mirror. Next was a bit unexpected as Matilda grabbed her tongue and lopped it off, in one smooth motion. Mother didn't have time to scream.

Shorty grabbed the needles and shoved them on the sides of both of her ears, quickly running the wire through. Pulling it tight, I heard her skin rip as her ears were pulled with wire to the back of her head.

Derek had come in with the grinder and was running it over her cheeks.

There was a step stool by her for me now. I painted her eyelids blue with paint, asking if she wanted a little shadow or a lot. She shook her head no. I added more. She tried to scream but she was all mumbles.

I ripped her fake lashes off her eyes, and applied a small amount of glue to them, sticking them back on.

"We're just getting started. Keep your eyes open and let me know if I'm doing anything right." It was my turn to sneer at her. I couldn't recognize her expression if I had needed to. She had no wrinkles and no expression, just a bit swollen.

I smeared red lipstick over her lips, going around them like a clown's. The Firebreather had heated a metal stick easy for me to handle, at his forge. Her eyes grew large despite the swelling when I brought the hot metal to her lips. I outlined them just like she had taught me, then filled in the lip with color. Red hot metal was the color. I hoped she liked it.

I decided against pulling her nails out. She had broken most of them in the struggle and a few of her nail beds were bleeding.

I called for Sander. He sent us all out of the tent and sent for his crew. We didn't have much time before Samantha's people showed up.

When the bonesaw came to life I heard grunts, then nothing more. I heard it come to life four times. Then nothing. The silence was loud.

CHP came running with heavy, waterproof bags. When Sander said we could come in, the tent was totally empty.

"Ready for round two. Go get cleaned up, Mia." He turned and walked out.

He was right, I looked a mess with paint, maybe a bit of blood on me. Samantha picked me up and ran with me back to the tent. We both needed to be ready for the next round, which was hers.

Samantha had been smart and had her clean clothes already set out. It didn't matter to me. Another long shirt, leggings, and sneakers were my plan.

Samantha took the clothes we had on and gave them to the Firebreather. They would disintegrate in his forge in no time. Whatever was left would be taken away by CHP.

CHP always knew of someone pouring a drilling pad or plugging a hole, to get rid of odds and ends like burnt up clothing.

Monroe was pounding on the wagon door. "Get ready for Round Two." He yelled.

Sideshow

I asked Samantha what her plan was. "I want to see if Dad recognizes me. When I told him, I felt like a girl, he beat me til I bled. He threatened to castrate me with the bulls if I brought it up again."

Samantha was crying and all I could do was hug her leg and offer a handkerchief. When she collapsed, to sit on the floor, I held and comforted her. I was patting her back and she burped, which was promptly followed by a fart.

"Looks like there's a bit of the old man still with me." We were both laughing tears.

"I know he won't accept me. I won't forgive him. He will lose his tongue, be castrated, then CHP can have all the flesh they want. No matter how rotten it is."

I gave Samantha a final hug and kiss on her cheek. "You should have shaved." I winked and we both laughed.

Monroe pounded on the door again. I opened it and tossed the clothes to him. "Come on already. Women-sheesh!" He was yelling but it didn't mean we would hurry any faster.

Samantha went into the tent I had been in earlier. There were two chairs, a work table off to the side of the tent with a few covered tools.

Sideshow

Chapter 14 Round Two

A couple of cups of coffee were set up with a beautiful silver setting, it reminded me of a high tea.

I told her to stay strong as I ducked under the bottom flap of the tent, where I lay down, waiting.

Samantha was sitting, drinking coffee when a man walked in. "And who are you supposed to be?"

Samantha set her cup down. "I am Samantha." Her voice did not waver. I was so proud of her.

"Boy, I told you, if you ever brought that shit up again, I'd castrate you and make you a girl myself." His voice was gruff and deep.

Samantha cleared her throat and stood tall. He was as tall as Samantha, way shorter than Matilda.

"Old man, the only castration which will happen here tonight, will be yours." I'd never heard Samantha speak with that cold tone, and honestly, it frightened me.

I saw Samantha shove him back in the chair. He looked shocked. His face was turning bright red. Even more when she punched him. His lights went out like a bulb on a Christmas tree.

In one swipe, she cleared the table with her hand, picked him up with the other hand and tossed him on the table like he weighed no more than a sack of flour. I think we all heard the hard grunt when he landed.

Samantha grabbed his pants leg and tugged them down, reached on the ground floor for the Burdizzo, a bloodless castration device, resembling pliers. Quickly applying them to him, I would swear I heard a crunch. He screamed.

Matilda quickly appeared to cut his tongue off.

"Wait!" Samantha's tone was sharp. "Do you have anything to say now? Now that you are less of a man?"

He spat in Samantha's face. Matilda grabbed his tongue and cut it off. You could see he was holding back tears. Who knew if they were from pain or remorse. I was guessing only pain.

Samantha was looking at him, shaking her head no. "Sander!"

Sander and his crew came in, sending Samantha and Matilda out. They made quick work of chopping off his arms and legs. The Firebreather was called in to cauterize the wounds. Before we knew it, the room was cleaned and ready for Derek's turn.

Derek was poking at a clump of weeds with his foot. I could see this was going to be a very emotional step for him. When he lifted his face to look at me, I didn't recognize him. His eyes looked almost glowing red.

"I want this over with, so I can be happy, hopefully with you." I held his hand and smiled.

Sander walked over to us with the Ringmaster and Monroe. "What's the plan?"

"Do we have time for coffee?" Derek sounded as tired as we all felt.

Monroe announced the last ones had not shown up yet, so we headed to the mess hall. Matilda saw us coming and started pouring coffee. It was silent for a few moments til Derek spoke.

"These people will not give me any more closure than the others did for the rest of you. *If* they even show up. My only request is to flog them first."

Derek took off his shirt and turned with his back toward us. There were scars on scars. He had been whipped. I gasped aloud, sure others did as well. He put his shirt back on.

Sideshow

He looked at me, then took my hands, apologizing for showing me. I put his hands to my lips, kissing first the left hand, then the right.

"Never apologize for showing me what life has done to you." Derek bent down and kissed me., then told of his plan.

"My plan is simple. Whip whoever comes in with a cat o' nine tails. Here is the one Mom and Dad took turns using on me. Use this on whoever, then take all the flesh you want. I'll meet with them momentarily, first."

Derek presented something looking like a whip, but the leather was shorter, in strands, with glass, rock and other hard, sharp objects attached by wire, or leather.

I felt sick. No wonder Derek's scars were so thick. We had all drunk about half of our coffee before the heads up was given by Grady that we had visitors in the parking lot.

Derek gave me a kiss then motioned for CHP and Monroe. Shorty picked up the whip.

"I'm doing this one, mate." Was all he said.

Derek nodded in agreement. I was guessing there was a history I didn't know yet. I wasn't sure if I should go to the tent or not, this time. Derek might need me, I took another drink and sat my cup down.

Sideshow

Chapter 15 Round Three

Derek was speaking with two people. I could only see one. Matilda and Monroe were nearby, so was CHP.

"Why did you summon us here, boy? You're the one we came to get. You're behind on your chores, and you'll be getting a whipping for worrying your Ma the way you did."

I'm guessing it was his mom and dad, in there with him. Derek was a dwarf while his parents were full sized. His mom was considerably shorter than his dad though.

"This isn't about me. I did all this for you." Derek sounded monotone, no emotion in his voice or in his body language.

About that time, Sander and the CHP crew walked in, grabbing his parents by their arms. His dad started screaming bloody murder. Matilda walked in and his jaw fell open. His mom looked at him and started crying. His parents didn't notice Shorty coming in.

"You're my son, how can you treat us so badly?" She started to wail with no tears falling.

"You're the one who treated me badly."

"Why you ungrateful little-" Shorty hit her back with the cat o' nine tails. She really did scream then.

His dad tried to take words back. "You know we didn't mean it, son. Just like you don't mean this. Just come home and things will be back to normal. After you receive your punishment for running off."

Shorty hit his back. The man didn't cry or scream. He stood there, his face turning all the shades of pissed off. Derek shook his head and Shorty hit them both again. His mom acted like she couldn't stand. His dad didn't say a word.

Shorty dropped the whip and walked out of the tent. Sander picked it up. "Boys."

Sander's boys made Derek's parents stand tall. "Anything else?"

His dad only glared at him, his mom wailing like she was dying. Well, not yet. Matilda reached over her, pulled her tongue out and cut it off. Then his dad screamed. Matilda stood in front of him. He wouldn't open his mouth. Derek held out the Burdizzo and his mouth opened. Matilda used the opportunity to grab his tongue and snipped it off. Once Matilda was out of the way, Sander motioned for everyone to leave the tent.

We could hear the cat o' nine tail making contact and ripping flesh. Sometimes there was a grunt but nothing else.

The bonesaw was fired up. We all walked back to the mess area to finish our coffee. Leaving CHP to the job.

Shorty had fresh coffee waiting for us when we returned, along with some finger sandwiches.

Matilda shook her head and laughed with Shorty. "It seemed like the day to make finger sandwiches." We tried to act surprised, but they really were good.

Sander joined us about an hour later. "Jobs are all done. We've been paid in full and then some."

I had to ask. No matter how much blood was on them, their makeup was still on, and their clothes had no signs of the day.

"Sander, if I may ask, how did you and your crew stay so clean throughout all that? I was a mess." I was hesitant in asking but he was laughing.

"What you see are our faces, not makeup. Our skin absorbs blood, which is why we require a pound of fresh flesh, for each of us to eat. We can go weeks without eating, but when we have an opportunity like this, our bodies store the food like camels store fatty tissue. What we don't want, the hogs clean up."

I wasn't certain if my finger sandwich would stay down, even if it was bologna and cheese. Not after learning of them eating fingers and everything else.

The Ringmaster stood, walking over to shake Sanders' hand. "Thank you for your services. I'm positive there will be more along the way."

Sanders waved goodbye, making eye contact with Derek, Samantha, and myself. We all waved back.

When the Ringmaster sat back down, he announced we would roll out tomorrow when everyone was ready. It was time to go home to the ranch.

Sideshow

Chapter 16 Homeward Bound

Shorty came over with another pot of coffee, filling our cups. "My vote is after breakfast. It will be hot ham and cheese sandwiches if everyone gets here early enough. Otherwise, it will be cold ham and cheese." Shorty was in a good mood today. Getting rid of some frustrations must have done him a world of good.

It was late, and I was ready to call it a night. Several others were yawning too. Derek walked me to the wagon, and I noticed Monroe walking Samantha to the wagon, holding her hand.

I nudged Derek and he said, "About time. Those two have been flirting for years." He winked at me. At the door, Derek stood me on the stairs and gave me a long kiss, which made my knees not too steady.

Samantha had picked Monroe up and stood him on the bench. He was giving her a kiss she'd never forget.

"Meet you for breakfast bright and early, Mia."

"At breakfast." Sigh.

I think both Samantha and I were love struck.

Sleep came easy, so did waking up to the sound of people waking up, hammers and tents falling, wagons idling. By the time Samantha and I were dressed and outside, the big top was down and being rolled. Most of the freaks lived in wagons, and they were lining up. The Performers had their trailers lined up, with some of them already gone.

The animals were being fed and ready for transport. They lived at the ranch on a semi-open range when not working.

Sideshow

Derek and Monroe were coming down the path toward us for breakfast. We walked in as couples, holding hands. Shorty was thanking his maker for something and smiling.

Over coffee and breakfast, Monroe asked if he could ride to the ranch with Samantha. The sword swallower would be driving his wagon to his home, which was on the way, where Monroe would take it over.

Before she could answer, Derek asked if I would ride in his wagon with him. He had made me a seat for a comfortable ride. How could I say no to that? I looked at Samantha, who was smiling and agreed. She agreed with Monroe.

We finished eating and helped Shorty finish storing plates and supplies. We were all ready to head to the ranch, and to a new life ahead.

Behind us, Sander and the CHP crew were waiting, for they knew that, before they were hungry, we would be ringing the dinner bell.

Katie Jaarsveld

Katie lives in the Netherlands with her husband and 2 cats.

When not spending time with her husband, pets, family and friends, she can be found engrossed in a favorite book, reviewing an Author's latest to be released or writing her next story.

You can read more from Katie in the following Anthologies:

Blood Pool in the Anthology MUTATE by Samie Sands.

The Unit, and My Skin Crawls are both in the Anthology ELECTROMAGNETISM by Samie Sands

Condemnation, Time Frame and From Death to Dust Bunnies are included in the anthology NIGHT MARES compiled by Samie Sands

Revenant's Welcome is in the anthology THIRTEEN Vol.3: The Never-Ending Nightmare by Kevin Hall

Time and Rewind is in the anthology It's Behind You compiled by Samie Sands

A Screen Across Ages is in the anthology THIRTEEN Vol.4 by Kevin Hall

Strange Behaviors is in the anthology Doomsday by Samie Sands

And Baby Makes… is in The Plus Sign, an anthology charity for Winchester Beacon of Hope Emergency Shelter

You can follow Katie at https://twitter.com/@KatieJaarsveld

Diamonique
Samie Sands

Dear Angelika,

Well, I've done it! I have finally achieved my goal in life. I've been accepted into the circus, so now my life is going to change…for the better.

Oh, it's so wonderful, sister, I wish you could see it through my eyes. I know mother thinks that the circus is something to be ashamed of, but I truly believe it to be a noble profession. I am around entertainers, people who make the world a more colorful place, who make people smile. They use their personalities and their skills to make people live happier lives, to give them a break from their mundane days.

How many people can say that?

Exactly, not many.

Oh, what a time to be alive! This explosive time period with all these amazing new opportunities. The world is becoming a thrilling place with entertainment at the center of it. Hollywood might have its role to play, but I am quite happy being here, thank you very much.

So, the freak show is interesting. I have met people, unlike anything I have ever seen before. The boy with crab claws for hands is fascinating. Good looking actually, a handsome man that would have women falling at his feet were it not for his strange hands that I have no idea how he copes with. Then there's the small woman. Mary. She is tiny and adorable, a real sweetie. Her height doesn't hold her back because she's such a tough cookie. I really admire her. There is also a lady with a beard. I do not know her name yet, but she is wonderful. She smiles all the time through the beard, which is very impressive.

There are other acts as well, trapeze artists, clowns, the performers who work with animals…they all do such a fantastic job. It really is a sight that the world is lucky to behold. When I watched the show for the very first time I thought my eyes were going to pop out of my head.

Can you imagine, me with no eyes? The best freak of them all!

I so wish you could see this world through my eyes. I think you would love this just as much as I do.

We will be moving soon, traveling to a new place, and I'm very excited about it. It will be scary to leave everything that I've ever known before behind, but I don't have the best memories in the world so maybe this is a good thing. I didn't realize how sheltered my existence was before I came here, but these people have seen it all, they aren't concerned with petty problems because they are out there having a good time. They have performed in parts of the world that I haven't even heard of.

That will be me soon, Angelika, I will be the one performing all over the world. Oh, what an exciting life I am going to have. I cannot wait for it.

Lots of love,
Your sister.
Diamonique.

Sideshow

Dear Angelika,

Life on the road is truly incredible, I don't know how to put it into words. Seeing the world, getting out of our small town, it's everything I hoped it would be and more. The places are beautiful, some of them green and colorful with nature as far as the eye can see, some of them gray with buildings all around, which can be a bit disconcerting…but it's all different, and that is better. Anything that isn't home is better for me.

The people are nice too…mostly. They come to our shows with wonder in their heart and an excitement to see something that they wouldn't normally see. A break from the mundane nature of their everyday lives. They 'ooh' and 'aah' at the animals, treating their trainers like they are gods. They watch the performers who can do crazy things with their bodies with wide eyes and happy expressions. The clowns are seen as funny little characters that might be found at the end of a child's bed, treated with child-like amusement.

Personally, I find the clowns quite terrifying. All that makeup…it makes me shudder. But I suppose it isn't like I'm going to find a clown at the bottom of my bed. Not unless I invite one…

Ooh, that probably made me sound really bad, didn't it?

I'm not like that. Not really. I never thought about that sort of thing before…but here, everyone is at it. It doesn't matter what anyone looks like, what their lives might be like, or what ailments they may or may not suffer, they are all enjoying one another's company. Even the freaks. Actually, they might be the worst of them all, I haven't decided yet.

Sideshow

Speaking of the freaks…they are the only people that I have seen be treated quite badly by the public. People act like they aren't human and that the vicious words which spill out of their mouths can't hurt them. They criticize the parts of them that haven't been afflicted badly, calling the boy with claw hands fat and mocking the bearded lady's dress sense, almost as if they get a kick out of making them feel bad about their life choices on top of everything else.

I always thought that I had a sheltered life, but at least I know that words spoken can have the most damaging effect of all. Physical injuries fade—and trust me, I have seen some of those dealt out too during my time traveling—but mental scars are the ones that will always last.

As for me? Well, right now I am observing all of this madness, enjoying the fun parts and doing what I can to ignore the bad. I am just one person, what difference can I make to the world? I am alone, trying to create a piece of entertainment. I do not have any power.

I'm sure it will be fine anyway. The world will slowly become a more tolerant place.

It has to, doesn't it?

Lots of love,
Diamonique.

Sideshow

Dear Angelika,

I am shaking. I do not know how I am managing to write in this state, it seems impossible. Yet I am so desperate to get these words out that somehow, I am finding a way.

Tonight, was not a good night, it was not a good show. Somehow, I knew that was going to be the case before we even got out there. I could feel something bad in the air as soon as we entered this town.

Maybe I could have told someone, I might've put a stop to this, but who would listen to me? I am still the new girl after all. Someone who hasn't been around for long enough to know how things really go. I knew that no one would listen to me, so I kept my fears to myself.

I don't know if I shall be doing that again, I have never experienced anything so terrifying in my life.

The crowd wasn't our usual, they were drunk and rambunctious before they even came near to us. Every single person seemed to have a glint in their eye, a desire for something that we definitely don't normally offer.

I did what I could to stay in the background, I didn't want anyone to notice me, yet that seemed to make me even more appealing to these people who turned out to be no better than animals.

Blood was shed tonight. One of the contortionists was killed and I heard some other terrible things happened to the girls who travel with us, I know I did not get it the worst by far…yet I have only been through my own experience, so I can only know how much that terrified me.

Four men grabbed me. They pulled me here there and everywhere, covering me with bruises. I can see the dots of purple and gray covering the skin of my arms now. They tried to tie me to a pole, but I fought like hell, kicking out with everything I have. A survival instinct told me that if I lost all the upper hand I would never be the same again.

I even bit one of the men, drawing blood.

That earned me a slap around the cheek, one that continues to sting with a red-hot heat now. But at least they stop trying to tie me up. They did tear my beautiful blue dress though and got a glimpse of my nipple.

Thankfully, I found some inner strength and I think that was you, sister. You helped me to fight, to survive, to get through the worst night of my life so far. So, for that, I have to thank you, Angelika.

We were going to stay here for another night, but thankfully now we have decided to move on. I don't have the heart to perform here again. I just couldn't do it.

I will be somewhere else when I write again and this time I hope it will be with good news.

Lots of love,
Forever grateful,
Diamonique.

Sideshow

Dear Angelika,

I am so afraid, this place that I hold so dear has become a torture chamber for me. It is the freaks, they are the ones that are causing all of this trouble. They have turned on everyone else, and each other too, blaming everyone for the way that things have gotten. For the hate that has been flung our way.

I do not believe that anyone is to blame for one bad show after another. Not inside the circus anyway. I think the outside world is to blame. Them and their small-minded views.

Maybe mother was right to say the things that she did. Perhaps she was correct about the world. I always assumed that her views were small town and that I knew better, but now I am not so sure.

There is evil in the world. True evil. I do not know how to get away from it.

Even as I sit here now, I am watching two of the freaks beat another nearly to death. I would like to intervene, to put a stop to this, but I am already regarded with disdain.

To be perfectly honest with you, Angelika, I am so afraid that I am next, that the freaks will turn on me. I say nothing because I do not want to be on the other end of that beating.

I do not want to die. Not out here, not like this.

I want to turn to the side and to be able to ask you what I should do, but I cannot.

In this, I am all alone.

I have never been given the opportunity to experience loneliness before. Not until now, and it hurts. I do not like it one bit. I understand why it is a choice for so many singers to sing about because it is a boundless emotion with so much to it.

This is made worse because I put myself in this situation. I chose this.

Angelika, I believe it might be time to go home, to go back to the life I left behind, the one that I was so desperate to escape. I might be bound here with a contract, but I have my own mind. If I wish to pursue other things I should be able to. No one else can tell me how to live my life...can they? Am I now a possession? Owned?

I do not sleep, I do not eat, I feel fear all the time. I think I have to leave otherwise I will simply fade away. I can already feel it happening, the color ebbing out of me. Like I already said, I do not want to die here. I want more for myself.

I need to take action, Angelika. In one way or another. First, I need to decide which way I want to go then I need to just do it.

You know me, once I have set my mind to something, nothing will stop me...that is what got me into this mess in the first place.

Yours,
Diamonique.

Sideshow

Dear Angelika,

I do not know what to say anymore. I am no longer keen on even writing to you because the news is so bad. There are bruises, all over my body, on parts of me that I have never wanted to be touched. My body is black and blue, red too. All over.

Can you even imagine what that feels like?

I suppose, maybe you can. It is not up to me to presume to know your experience.

Things have happened to me, sister, things I do not ever wish to remember again. Yet every single time I close my eyes, there it is, happening to me over and over.

This world is not glamorous, it is not entertainment in the way that I presumed it would be. It is deadly and dangerous, nightmarish to the core. I do not understand why anyone would wish this upon themselves.

Everyone from the circus is entertainment to the outside world, but as a prop, a toy, rather than a human being. They do not have one shred of decency towards us, as the mess of my body shows.

You have had experiences with the opposite sex too, haven't you, Angelika? I do hope it did not feel to you the way that it did to me.

They say when you experience trauma that you should be able to escape in your mind. Your brain should protect you and take you somewhere beautiful, but that is not the experience that I have had. That is because the world is not a beautiful place.

The world is ugly, sister, it is filled with something so hideous I cannot even find the words for it. I hate it. I **hate** it. I cannot explain to you the hate I feel. It is as if a beast, a fiery hot red demon, has crawled within me and it wants to break free, to do some real damage, to rid the world of its ugliness.

It knows how to do it as well.

I have a blade, Angelika. I am twisting it between my fingers as I speak. I know with utter certainty that I need to take revenge on the world, to rid it of this ugliness. It is my purpose. I do not know how I understand this, but I do. It is what I have been put here for. I do not have any choice in my actions.

But who do I take revenge on?

The freaks who fight among themselves, who blame the world for their issues, who are aesthetically ugly? Or the men with true evil lying in their hearts? They might look beautiful to the outside world, but there is something truly disgusting inside of them?

I know this must scare you, sister, and I am truly sorry for that. But this is what I must do.

Blood will be shed, you mark my words. The next time you hear from me, I will have made a difference to this place.

Your sister forever,
Diamonique.

Sideshow

Angelika,

Red. All I see is red, as far as the eye can see.

It is good though. This red. It is cleansing.

Maybe I went too far. Perhaps I killed too many. I certainly feel very weak with it all. My arm is aching, not wanting to move. My writing might be too scruffy for you to read.

Not that you will be reading this anytime soon.

I can tilt my head now and see you clearly, for the very first time ever. Yet I am as lonely as I have always been. You have always made me feel this way, like I have no one in the world, which has only gotten worse since we made this decision. To join the circus.

Or *you* made the decision. As the head attached to your body with only the control of one arm, I have never been able to make any choices for myself. I pretend to myself, and you in these letters, that I am strong and independent, able to do as I please, but that is all falsehood.

I presume you think yourself to be so much better than me because you have always had the power.

Maybe you are.

However, *you* are the one who wanted to come here, to call us a freak, and to join in with the others. *You* wanted to remain when it was clear that everyone thought a two-headed woman disgusting. *You* chose to have sex. They were all terrible choices and I was only along for the ride.

I am the one who cleansed this world, who made it better than it already is. *I* am the one who surprised everyone by going on a rampage and ridding the world of the ugliness. I killed the disgusting men with their lewd intentions, the freaks who do not know how to conduct themselves, the owner of this circus, who makes pain from our misery...

And I killed my biggest enemy too.

You.

I slashed your neck, twisted my arm to plunge the blade into your head, and I twisted until we existed in a river of red, and now finally, you are gone. You cannot plague me with your bad choices again.

Only my worst enemy was also me. You are my organs, my heart, my blood, my life force. Taking out you will also destroy me. I do not have any choice in that. Again, you have taken the power away from me. But still, I feel good about my decision. Even as my eyelids grow heavy and my writing illegible, I know that this was the right thing to do.

Mother will never understand, I do not believe that she ever understood anything we have done. She will move on with her life though, probably with relief. Her burden is no more. We are gone, she no longer has to deal with the knowledge that she could not even produce a normal child. I hope she finds happiness in this ugly world.

This is over now, just as it should be.

The conjoined twin, the two-headed girl, is no more.

The end,
Diamonique.

Samie Sands

Samie Sands is the author of the **AM13 Outbreak series**, published by Limitless Publishing. She's also had short stories included in **Amazon bestselling anthologies** and work featured on **Wattpad**.

To follow Samie's work, please connect with her online:
Website: samiesands.com
Facebook - /SamieSandsLockdown
Twitter - @SamieSands

Heaven Must Be Missing An Angel

Andrew Darlington

*An encounter with a rough-sleeper
leads to complications…*

She was crying. She was sitting on folds of cardboard on the street, crying. She was sitting on the corner just down from St Pancreas Station, on folds of cardboard, crying. Writhing from side-to-side, as though in physical pain, sobbing softly. I watch her. People stream by taking no notice, talking into mobiles, talking to each other, dragging their wheeled cases. Human suffering here on the street, and we're too caught up in living even to glance. Another derelict on another corner. Another casualty. I toss a two-pound coin that dances and spins on the pavement.

I walk a little further to the British Library courtyard. Sit on the perimeter wall and consider her. Deep in thought for long moments. People drift up and down the wide Library steps. People pore over laptops, talking America. Pigeons scratch and fuss around flakes of dropped 'Greggs' sausage rolls.

Eventually, I retrace my steps. Past the busker and the 'Big Issue' seller. Uber cabs and tourist coaches shush past. And she's still there.

I crouch down beside her. "Are you alright?" Which is a dumb question, because she's obviously not alright.

She wipes tears and almost smiles. Slightly pretty behind the straggly black hair. Big wide eyes as deep as black holes. Mid-to-late twenties, no more. Her brown coat pulled in close around a faded floral-print dress.

"Hungry?"

No-one even glances as I lead her into the burger bar and guide her to the corner alcove. She dumps her pack on the floor. I get two cappuccinos. Her hands, tipped by grimy fingernails, lace tight around the glass as though intent on drawing its warmth into her. She wolfs the burger as I watch.

"Virgil, Virgil Caine is my name" I say. "What's your name?"

She says what sounds like "Anna", thickly accented, around chewing mouthfuls. Eastern European. She smiles again, warily, through her hair. I try a few more questions, but she either doesn't understand or pretends she doesn't understand. Her words could be Romanian or Polish. I don't know enough Polish to tell for sure. Could I believe her anyway? If she could tell me her tale, can I believe anything? The way she was writhing on the street betrays substance dependency. But then, sleeping rough needs numbing solace. It's so easy. She could weave sympathy-stories of people-trafficking, an escape from sexual slavery, and I'd be none the wiser. They have ways of tapping into your good nature until you can never be certain of anything.

Sideshow

I ask her where her parents are. I ask where she comes from. I ask if there's anywhere she can go…if she has family or friends. She shrugs and says nothing. After all, isn't the street the place you go to forget how to find yourself? But when she does speak, a brief phrase, then a little more, I understand none of it.

She settles back into the seat, wiping her fingers on the folded branded paper napkin. I can see the tracks of her tears down the side of her snub nose. There's a sprinkling of freckles. Has she suffered abuse? There are small healing scabs beneath her right eye, and across the bridge of her nose. Or is it an eczema-type infection, due to poor diet? Soft electro-jazz swirls around us from some unseen device. On other tables, people gorge carelessly, so much thoughtless food indulgence. Such obscene gluttony amid casual wealth, while others sleep on the streets. It's grotesque, illogical, it makes no sense. She raids the plastic cup for packets of sugar, white and brown, and stuffs them deep into her pockets. Glances across at me as though sharing a conspiracy. I wonder what she has in her bag. A change of underwear? A book? Tampons?

When I start up to leave, she makes to follow. As though we are now a unit. The problem of spontaneous generosity is that it implies obligation. A follow-through that's difficult to tactfully discourage. Should I just give her money? And if so, how much? What will be an acceptable amount, without appearing either tight-fisted or an easy touch? Or will that simply leave a guilty backwash, as though she'll think of it as conscience money? She follows me to the bus stop, I swipe my card for her fare and she sits opposite me on the coach all the way to Tooting High Street. Once there, I help her down onto the pavement.

112

Sideshow

There's a cool breeze. There's always a cool breeze here. Even the light is flat and hard.

At times I feel a strange detachment from all this. As though I'm watching it from outside, from someplace immeasurably remote, beyond time and space. Untouched by the squalid tragedy of it all.

We walk in the direction of Amen Corner but turn off into the narrow streets where green wheelie-bins sit in predatory formation. Along Oriental Terrace, there's garbage crushed into the paving cracks and graffiti on the walls. I'm old enough to remember when things were different. When people had pride and took care. I unlatch the door and she follows me inside, dumping her bag in a pile beside the sofa. She looks around in a vaguely disapproving way, as though she expected more. A bigger TV perhaps, or a Sky-box?

I make my excuses, go into the kitchen and check the kettle. I allow the tap to run. Then fill the water-filter. While it purifies the impurities from the water, I rummage through the drawers beside the sink, where I keep tea-towels, dusters, candles, scourer-pads, matchboxes, and coils of washing line.

Anna barely struggles as I loop the cord around her neck and apply pressure. She just gives a resigned moan. As though she understands and accepts what I offer. We should never live our lives imprisoned by fear, we should reach out and embrace its potential. Her body bucks and writhes, as they all do. But eventually quietens. Into a perfect stillness. I carry her upstairs. A weightless thing. I undress her reverently. The soiled clothes will be laundered and ironed. She's painfully thin and undernourished, with small undeveloped breasts. I run the water in the bath, monitoring its warmth with my hand—not too hot or too cold, running perfumed gel into a layer of foam. Lower her into the water, and sponge her clean, ritually cleansing away the street-grime, using moist cotton-wool to tease away the small abrasions around her nose, shampooing and rinsing her straggly hair, brushing it and combing it into shape.

I towel her dry with a big fluffy white towel, clothe her in one of the long white nightdresses that I keep in the wardrobe, just in case, and lay her out on the bed. Then use cosmetics to make up her face in subtle shades, nothing too vulgar. Her nails had been broken and grimy, I varnish them into respectability. The same with her neat toenails. I stand back with a catch in my throat. She looks beautiful. She deserved better, someone to care enough to free her. But where no-one else cared, I've rescued her from dirt and pain, cruelty and terror.

I sit in the chair beside the bed, watching her. Later, I'll enter her safely in the garden, where the world can longer hurt her.

Alongside the others.

Andrew Darlington

Ho-Hum. Probably all this has been provoked by other aspects of my own writing. Because meanwhile, my "The Strange Death Of Sherlock Holmes" story is now in the new 'Mammoth Book Of Sherlock Holmes Abroad' (edited by Simon Clark) anthology—into which I've added a time travel element provoked by the thought that Doyle's tales were appearing in 'The Strand' simultaneously with the serialization of Wells' 'The War Of The Worlds' in 'Pearsons'. We'll see where it takes us. Oddly, I wrote two stories. The first, "The Beast Of The Baskervilles" was bounced because it didn't actually feature Sherlock Holmes himself, only elements of his mythos. It wound up in the 'Tigershark' online magazine.

Find out more at http://andrewdarlington.blogspot.co.uk/.

Stuff of Dreams
Rick Eddy

When I was a young boy my mother would berate my father when he allowed me to stay up late and watch the Friday "Fright Night" horror movie on local television. This was because the movie always gave me nightmares. My father slept through these, but they ruined my mother's good night's sleep, as she always got up to console me in my nighttime ravings. Every Friday for several years of my childhood, I was found riveted to the black-and-white TV screen, gobbling up popcorn and soaking up the dreadful deeds of Dracula, the Frankenstein monster, the Mummy or some other televised fiend. Giant spiders, alien invaders, and bug-eyed monsters also made their appearances, but rarely affected me deeply. However, the more human-like the creature—Karloff embodying reanimated flesh or the hypnotic stare of the arch-vampire Lugosi—the more terrified and visceral my reaction. Once asleep, a bizarre but realistic replay of the film would be projected inside my suggestible head, wrenching me awake with thrashing, screaming, and disorientation. These were true, palpable and harrowing nightmares that shook me to the core. It took me a while to outgrow this pattern, at least several months or more, but I'm sure it seemed like years to my mother. Since it never bothered dear old dad, we kept watching the creature features together in a subliminal bonding experience that I have since passed on, consciously or otherwise, to my own offspring in turn.

Sideshow

Dad was always a fan, even an advocate, of the strange, the offbeat and the bizarre. His bookshelves held not only many works of H.P. Lovecraft, William Hope Hodgson and other purveyors of the weird and fantastic, but also fact-based volumes such as "Anomalies and Curiosities of Medicine" and illustrated histories of surgery and dissection. By profession, my father was a biologist who found a niche as a medical technologist specializing in hematology. As such he was interested in the interplay between the biological and the metaphysical; fascinated by the nebulous region between the natural and the supernatural. His enjoyment of the classic "monster movies" was one manifestation of this. He explored how and when the human became inhuman, and vice versa. On camping trips, he would tote along several paperbacks about unnatural beings and abnormal experiences. By the campfire he would recite otherworldly tales that were just believable enough to make the dancing of the flames, sparking and popping of the burning wood and the usual nighttime noises of the outdoors seem to open up some shadowy realm in which human transfiguration might take place.

Of all the aspects of my father's preoccupation with the weird and unusual, perhaps nothing was more emblematic than his dedication to the sideshow at the local county fair. In my childhood years, the local fair always opened towards the end of August, so it came to herald the waning of the hot season and the coming of the inevitable decay of fall. The fair was a final fling with summer, and I always tried to maximize the experience with an overdose of fried food, soda pop, popcorn, and cotton candy. It was usually a family affair, with my mother and older brothers all visiting the various stalls and attractions together. Then my father would break off to take my two older brothers to see the sideshow, which I understood to be a polite term for "the freaks." I would stay with my mother, feeling cheated again by my age, wondering what mysteries lurked in those ragged tents down the midway.

Sideshow

I had to make do with the other activities available to the younger set. The fair provided many highlights, including ribbon-festooned horses, cows, pigs, and other farm animals; amusement rides and games awarding winners with stuffed animals and cheap plastic toys, and the usual Hall of Mirrors and Haunted House attractions. None of these could compete, however, with the truly mind-bending things that were rumored to be found behind the facades and inside those last tents at the end of the midway. They were peculiar and awful things, darkly hinted at but never named. Having not yet witnessed these oddities I was left only to imagine what might be living and breathing down that dusty, straw-strewn path.

One late August visit—I must have been eleven or twelve—my father said I was ready to take in the sideshow. My older brothers were no longer interested in the fair. Over my mother's objections, Dad and I ambled off on what was for me a new adventure. I felt queasy in my stomach as I contemplated what sights I might soon see. Dad contemplated the freak show with a grain of salt, telling me calmly that "freaks" by definition usually equaled fakery, while at the same time telling me I would be amazed, if not downright terrified, by what I would see. He said the sideshow offered unique deformities and monstrosities that were certain to satisfy the most curious student of the strange and bizarre. He couched his interest in the objects of the sideshow with scientific jargon and measured hypotheticals, leaving just enough room for a young boy's imagination to fill in the blanks: Why couldn't a woman grow a beard? What could cause a man to develop scales like a lizard? When was a being no longer a human?

The first few exhibits were relatively tame, as if they were offered as mere appetizers to the realm of the weird. There were feats of strength and flexibility, remarkably under-dressed women with astonishing endowments, and displays of fire-eating and sword-swallowing. Farther down the line were even stranger sights, such as the Human Pincushion, pierced with nails all over his body; the Wolf Boy, covered from head to toe with thick fur;

and the Living Skeleton, the thinnest man on earth whose vertebrae could be seen through the skin of his belly. But in the last couple of tents lurked some profoundly hideous examples of human degradation that had been turned into marketable commodities by fellow human beings.

As we approached those last tents my father cautioned me not to be shocked, but to leave the tent if I couldn't stand to look. These were, after all—he solemnly reminded me—still human beings. Most of all, he said, I was not to scream, shout, laugh, cry or act out in any way, since they deserved our compassion as much as they might elicit our astonishment—or even nausea. His warnings only heightened my sense of anxiety and anticipation.

The first display of distorted humanity was "Wanda the Armless Wonder." She was propped at a tiny dining table, going through the normal motions of eating a meal, except that she had no arms. Her legs, feet, and toes fulfilled all the functions of the usual appendages. She fed herself adroitly, with no sign of clumsiness or unease, a beatific smile upon her face. I noticed that she made no eye contact with any of us who passed by to observe her impressive demonstration of deft but unusual table manners.

Next to Wanda's scene was "Kontorto the Rubber Band Man." He was positioned on a platform, feet facing forward with his spine curved so far back so as to have his head and face peeking out from between his legs. The proximity of his face to his crotch was deeply disturbing and conjured up strange notions in my pre-pubescent mind. He also had a glassy, far-off stare that suggested his mind was anywhere but connected to the extreme position into which his body was twisted.

The next tent housed a truly repulsive example of the depths to which humans could descend. This abominable creature was billed as "A Genuine Geek—Eats And Does Anything—For A Quarter!" My father whispered the general definition of a "geek:" a particular kind of freak known to eat live animals. Dressed in soiled jeans and a grimy T-shirt stained with what looked like blood, the floor around the geek was littered with the partially-devoured bodies of snakes, rats, and other unidentifiable things. Dozens of quarters were strewn among the animal wreckage. I was disgusted, but my father forced a smile as we passed by the scenario, not quite averting our eyes.

The final tent advertised that this exhibit "Must Be Seen To Be Believed!" This was the "Unique, One-and-Only!" display of "The Incredible Living Head!!!" Once inside the tent, we were surrounded by shadows created by an array of thick curtains. It took several moments for our eyes to adjust to the dim surroundings. A grating voice from a tinny loudspeaker squalled out an introduction to ". . . a most gruesome human anomaly, a genuine medical miracle, a woman who should be dead yet somehow lives!" The build-up to the exhibition continued with an elaborate pseudo-medical explanation about what we were about to see: "Saved By A Team Of International Surgeons!!! Kept Alive On The Border Between Life And Death!!!" Then an inner curtain parted, and we beheld a large cylindrical tank of greenish water resting on a table, a skirt of fabric covering the space from the table to the floor. In the tank, about half the size of a 55-gallon drum, was a woman's head suspended on the surface of the liquid. It was supported by a floating plastic base from which dangled several wires and tubes that trailed off into the cloudy, opaque depths of the tank. I searched eagerly but in vain for any hint of the rest of her body. Only the head could be seen.

The woman—that is, the head—was clearly alive: she smiled, moved her eyes, winked deliberately and even made furtive kissing motions with her pursed ruby-red lips. In fact, I was certain she had looked at me directly, slowly batting her eyelashes, then blowing me an obviously suggestive kiss. In my young, under-developed sense of maleness, I was galvanized at some primal core of my being. I gazed upon her ghastly form and hideous circumstances, this creature-not-fully-human. I found myself curiously moved in my guts and my heart—in one word, aroused. It was a dizzying and disorienting combination of emotions. As I gaped at the spectacle my mind raced with thoughts of what kind of attraction this was, and how I could be so affected by both what was visible and what was invisible.

My father led me out of the tent, chuckling to himself, apparently amused by the confused look upon my face. He remarked that this last one was really "something to see," and rambled on about "lighting" and "mirrors" and "angles." I avoided eye contact with him, afraid that my infatuation with the disembodied head would somehow reveal itself upon my face. We walked back through the midway past the other attractions of the fair, met up with my mother, and headed to our parked car. We were quiet on the way home, my father asking every few minutes if I was alright. I nodded and murmured that I was fine. My mother, equally inquisitive, met with the same minimal response. I remained preoccupied and lost in my thoughts once we arrived at home. Mercifully, my parents didn't pry into my reactions or feelings and left me alone in those thoughts for the evening.

That night I had a dream unlike any I had ever experienced before. Instead of the horrific nightmares I had endured up to that point, I was visited by visions of a voluptuous young woman swimming in crystal clear blue water. In the dream, my point of view was oddly in continuous motion, and my sight of her expanded, diminished, and enlarged as if rotating within a kaleidoscope. At one moment I could observe her entire body in multiple miniatures; in the next, I could see only a single close-up of her crimson lips. In the clarity of the water, she would spin and twist and turn, lithe muscles rippling and shining with the palpable exertions. She paused and stared and smiled at me. Then her head abruptly separated from her body; she vanished, and the surrounding water instantly dissipated, leaving wires, tubes, separators, forceps, scalpels and other surgical implements scattered on a sodden floor. I woke up with a start in the middle of the night, heart racing and short of breath. I was alone in the darkness and stillness of my bedroom, besieged by alien emotions and bedeviled by strange bodily excitements.

Sideshow

Neither our father-son talks nor the books I had consulted about my changing pubescent body had prepared me for the bewildering array of sensations I was experiencing. This was my own journey into that territory between the physical and the immaterial, the empirical and the emotional. I had entered my own numinous state of transition, no longer a child but not yet fully a man. I was more than just a body, even as my body was redefining me.

This is my memory of that long-ago August evening. From that point on I was a new person, having shed the naive innocence of childhood as a newer identity emerged. I had a new appreciation for what makes us truly human. My experience in that disturbing sideshow tent never gave me nightmares, but instead became the stuff of dreams.

Rick Eddy

Rick Eddy is an ordained Lutheran minister with a background in mental health and human services. He has served variously as a pastor, prison counselor, foster care and child protective worker over several decades. Currently he's working to translate some of his life experiences into poetry and short stories. Some of his influences are Universal and Hammer horror films, The Twilight Zone and The Book of Revelation. Although a native of Western New York, he has lived in several different regions of the US as well in Sweden, and considers himself a citizen of the world.

WONDERLAND
Samie Sands

I force my eyes open, grabbing onto my throbbing head as I do so. Where am I again? I push my aching body up from the hard ground that lies beneath me. It takes a while for my sight to fully return, the blinding light making it almost impossible to see anything surrounding me. I rack my brain, trying to remember anything that might help me figure out what's going on, but nothing comes. Not even my name. How do I not even know my own name? That's impossible. I pat my head gently, trying to shake something in there, but the movement only makes me feel worse. Nausea overcomes me and I bend forward gasping for air.

My legs feel weak as I try to bear all of my weight on them. I stagger back against the cold stone wall and my head droops forward, my eyes rolling towards the ground. Water droplets fall and hit the ground with a resounding splash. I don't know if they are tears or just an irritation of my retina. I hope it's the latter, crying is the last thing I need to be doing right now. When the blurriness clears slightly, I can see that I am wearing some very strange silver gladiator sandals on my feet. I wiggle my toes, just to check that the vision *is* really me. Then my eyes continue to travel up my body to see what else I have on. I am shocked by the navy-blue jumpsuit covering my body.

Sideshow

I hate it.

I mean, I literally hate it. I don't know how old I am, or what I'm called, but I *do* know that I despise this outfit. What on earth would possess me to even think of putting this on? I was obviously way off with my first impression that this was all just a bad hangover. I would not be seen *dead* on a night out in anything this hideous. I let out a deep sigh and start focusing on movement. I can't exactly stand here, in this tiny unfamiliar room all day. The pure white interior is driving me to distraction, it's almost suffocating me. Hopefully, my memories will all come flooding back when I work out where this is.

I lean tentatively out of the doorway and am faced with a long, white corridor which seems to go on forever. A million possibilities fly uncontrollably through my brain, but I don't allow myself to focus on any particular idea. None of them are very pleasant. I try not to let the fear that is bubbling away in my stomach consume me entirely, and keep my mind focused on each small movement that I can get my body to make. Slowly, my limbs begin to loosen up and move more naturally. The relief that floods through me at that moment is halted when I hear voices behind me.

I quickly spin around; all of my defenses are sky high. I feel silly as I realize my fists have automatically risen above my face, but luckily no one is there to see it. My hands flop dejectedly down to my side as my ears prick up, trying to latch on to any more sounds. Noises mean people, which I am hoping will lead to answers. The laughter continues and I nervously follow it. I try and tell my heart rate to slow down, that there is nothing to be afraid of, but it hammers away noisily nonetheless. I eventually find myself outside a room very similar to the one I have just left. Inside I can see two boys sat close together in the corner of the room.

Their backs are to me and they are so engrossed in something that they're looking at they don't even notice me standing there.

I let out an awkward cough, unsure of how I should get their attention. One of them turns sharply and growls at me. I can't immediately speak as I drink in his appearance. He is pale, thin and very small. He is hunched over so tightly that I'm sure he must be frozen that way. His dark hair matches his eyes exactly, which gives him a sinister twist, one that sends iciness up and down my spine. I'm also fascinated by the paper hat perched on the top of his head. What is that all about?

Before another sound can pass by my lips, movement catches the corner of my eye. The other boy has risen and is now stood in front of me, smiling brightly. He pushes his hand into mine and starts shaking it vigorously, almost painfully. When he begins shouting, a possibility I didn't even *consider* before pops unwelcomingly into my thoughts.

"Bill!"

Is this…?

"My name!"

It can't be.

"I'm called Bill!"

Could this be some sort of mental institution? Is everyone here crazy? Does that mean *I'm* crazy? I don't *feel* crazy, should I know that I'm crazy? This isn't fair. I don't want to be stuck here in a nut house surrounded by weirdoes. Especially when I don't even know why.

"Bill, what is this place?"

I finally speak up. My speech is gravelly and my throat stings with each word. I almost feel as if my voice box has been left unused for a very long time. I try and cough again to clear it, but this only results in it feeling much worse. I don't really hold out much hope for a decent answer, but I figured it can't hurt to try. His reaction absolutely stuns and confuses me. He immediately backs away with his hands partially covering his face. The sheer panic in his eyes suggests to me that his silence comes from a much deeper place than idiocy. His mouth opens and closes rapidly like a goldfish. He retreats back into the corner and slumps to the ground. Both the boys proceed to take up a rocking motion, their expressions glazing over. As much as I try and talk or shake them out of this state, they do not move. It's as if I no longer even exist to them. I pull back and watch them for a further thirty seconds before giving up and moving on, shrugging my shoulders as if I'm not at all bothered by this creepy place. Inside my brain is screaming at me, but I don't give up the relaxed demeanor. I just have a strange *feeling* that someone, somewhere is watching me, wanting me to react.

As I leave the room, I walk smack into identical twins. Two girls, both very blonde, very slim with curves in all the right places and unbelievably gorgeous. Jealousy raises its ugly head straight away, how come I have to wear this hideous sack, but these two get to grace the halls in jeans and skin-tight t-shirts? I bet their beauty has given them some sort of power and control. I start to think that I am not in a mental home, after all, these girls appear perfectly normal to me. But then they start to talk.

"You should avoid those boys…"

They say this in perfect unison, pointing into the room with *exactly* the same movements. It's creepy, like something out of a horror film. Uneasiness spreads through my entire body. Somehow, I just know that this is all worse than I first thought. Something terrible is going on here.

Sideshow

"You don't want to get mixed up with...the *wrong* people."

They continue talking at me, unaware of my distrust of them. Everything about them is the same; there isn't one distinguishing feature between them. They look more like robots, or two puppets being pulled by the same strings. I scan my eyes, trying to find some evidence that they aren't actually human, but can't seem to spot anything unique. When they start manically laughing, something very strange happens. A memory. Well, I *think* it's a memory. A flash of something runs through my mind. A group of girls, all very similar in appearance to these two, all in perfect proportion with no ugly feature about them. They are all laughing and pointing at something. Their laughter doesn't sound unkind, but I can somehow tell that there is a malicious nature about the whole event. Before I can pick anything out, before I can even make any decisions about what I'm seeing, it's gone.

I shake my head wildly, trying to get it back. I want to grasp onto that memory, I want to claim it, to turn it into something more. I'm so desperate to remember everything that I forget for a moment where I am. The twins are frozen on the spot, both staring blankly at me. I walk up closer to them, waving my hand in front of their eyes to no reaction. It's happened again, I don't exist to them anymore. I touch their skin, expecting a metallic feel; I've almost convinced myself that they're robots. But no, they are as soft to touch as I am. Although my skin is much more blemished than these two. I compare my arms to the nearest twin to me and where she is porcelain; I am patchy, red and covered in deep welts. The confusion within me starts to transfer to anger and frustration.

I walk on, following the direction that the twin's frozen

bodies were pointing to, a determination and purpose in every single step. Rage is pushing me on, I deserve to know what exactly I'm doing here, I need to know why I'm hurt and no one else seems to even be *real*. The corridor goes on for such a long time, I'm certain I have been walking for over an hour and not a single thing has changed. I could be going around in circles for all I know. Each room I pass is empty, I haven't seen a soul. Why is that? If this really is a hospital, shouldn't there be someone, a doctor, a nurse? Anyone would do. Someone who could just explain everything to me. I try again to remember anything about myself, about anything that happened before here, but my mind remains blank. Even the memory from before is fuzzy and interchangeable.

To my delight, the next thing I spot up ahead is a circle of light. A door leading to the outside world. My spirits soar as everything else melts away. Nothing matters if I can escape this place. If I can get outside these walls, I'm sure I'll somehow find a way home, which will be *full* of clues to my life. Whatever is going on here won't matter when I've escaped; I can just forget ever setting foot in here. I'll be glad to. The tight knot in my stomach loosens as I spot sky and grass. I'm really going to be free. I pick up the pace to a jog, all the time trying to convince myself that the sensation that something is behind me, wanting to trap me inside is all in my imagination.

The door swings open very easily and I let out the breath that I didn't even realize I was holding. I didn't want to consider the possibility that it would be locked, and now I don't have to. The fresh air rushes into my lungs, almost filling me up entirely, while a strange sight flashes before my eyes. A small child is skipping playfully, singing cheerfully. But in the next instance, the same child is laying on the ground, covered in blood and dirt and screaming out in agony. The change in mood is so dramatic, and without the middle section of the story, it is impossible to work out why and what happened. I don't *feel* like the child is me, I feel really disconnected from the entire scene, so I don't know why I'm thinking about it now.

Before I can get too sucked in by my odd thoughts, I notice a pair of eyes lazily staring in my direction. I am so surprised to finally see another person that I stand in the same spot smiling for, what feels like, an eternity. He looks only slightly older than me, but frail and disheveled as if he has recently been through some very turbulent times. He is holding a white stick between his fingers, which he moves sensually up to his lips. A strong craving is awoken within me, and I find my legs moving me towards him lustfully. I sit down next to him, not breaking eye contact for even a second. I tilt my head slightly and purse my lips, moving towards him. Everything within me is screaming out for his touch. I desperately want his fingers to grace my skin.

Just before we connect, I snap backward breaking the spell. The earthy smelling smoke which is rising from the object within his hands grabs my attention. I realize with a start that I want *that*, not him. This boy isn't what I desire; it's the overly familiar thing that he's smoking. I reach out to touch it, but he slaps my hand away violently. The sudden change in his demeanor stings almost as sharply as the red mark starting to make its appearance on my skin. I feel like I should say something, I want to clear the air a bit to change the awkwardness that hangs in the air like a knife dangling above my head, but what can I do? I don't even know who *I* am, never mind who this boy is. I don't know how to act, how to resolve things with a stranger.

Sideshow

Sensing my internal struggle, the boy waves his fingers above his head in a circular motion. Puzzled, I look around at what he is showing me and I'm faced with a grim reality. I haven't escaped at all; the building is all around me. In fact, from what I can is it goes on for miles and miles. I can't see anything except twisted brick buildings for as far as the eye can see. This looks like the only fresh air I will be getting for a very long time. I look back at him, desperation evident in all of my features, panic obvious in my eyes. He shrugs despondently and turns away from me. Before I can lose him as well, I pull him roughly to look up at me.

"Please?"

I whisper quietly in case he isn't allowed to tell me anything. He shakes his head sadly and starts to turn again. I grab his collar and stare at him defiantly. That's when he opens his mouth and I see why he can't talk. There is a large empty gap where his tongue should be. Someone has removed his ability to speak. They've simply…cut it out. I drop him as if he's on fire and jump to my feet. Sick rises in my mouth and I slap my palms across my lips to stop any spilling out. What the fuck is going on? What sort of sick, twisted place does that to people? More importantly why?

The next thing I am aware of, I am back inside and sprinting down another corridor. My chest is tight and I can barely breathe so I force my body to stop. As it does, it collapses to the ground, unable to move even the slightest amount. I have no idea how I have kept running when I am obviously so shattered. This place has done some weird things to me and my body. I lie still, panting heavily letting everything I *do* remember play itself over and over again. I don't know how it's possible to not know anything about myself. I don't even know if the flashes of memory that I keep experiencing are even mine. They could be being somehow placed within me. Is that possible? I really don't know. I don't feel like I know anything anymore.

I wonder how I got here. I think about who I could have been before all of this. Did I have a family? Friends? A job? A life? How can someone just *forget* everything about themselves? The room swirls around me; the blank white walls become something different, more colorful. Lights flicker on and off, carnival music begins playing. My mind is tricking me into believing something that isn't there. None of this is logical, or even plausible. Things don't just *change* before your eyes, that just doesn't happen.

I close my eyes and embrace the blackness. I don't want to see anything else that my crazy mind or this weird place has to offer. I just want to sleep. I want my thoughts to become dreams, reality and fantasy to blur then I can blame all of this on something else. As I drift, fate seems to decide that it has other ideas for me and booming noises echo out from every angle. I jump up shocked, my heart racing and my palms sweating. The headache that was beginning to subside is now back with full force, and it thumps along merrily with the pounding music that is now blaring.

A boy enters my peripheral vision and I am immediately struck by what an odd character he seems to be. He is hopping from foot to foot, talking to his hand whilst his eyes flicker rapidly from side to side. His clothes are scruffier than I have seen on anyone so far and I wonder why that is. Outfits appear to be linked to status in here. Then again, that could just be me attaching meaning to something that doesn't exist. Who knows, maybe I have always been obsessed with fashion. I screw up my nose, I can't *imagine* I'm that shallow, but of course, I can't exactly be sure. As I watch him, the music and the lights seems to become much louder and more intense. It's as if a dream sequence is rapidly descending into a horrific nightmare. I push my fingertips into my ears, trying to block the noise out, trying to focus. I'm pretty sure that I need my wits about me if I intend to get out of here alive.

I spin around and everything shrinks, then grows, then changes all over again. I feel sick, I feel dizzy and I didn't know it was possible to feel so terrified. Even when this place *looks* nice, it has a sinister atmosphere. I refuse to be fooled. I can't ever let my guard down. A running track materializes, complete with a stout man holding a starting gun. A braying crowd starts to close in on me, I feel like some of them are actually yelling in my ears, even though they are so far away from me that I can't make out any of their faces.

A shrill ringing emanates from the strange boy and his hopping instantly stops. He holds a phone in front of his face as if someone is about to jump out from it and murder him. I stare at him, mesmerized until he eventually answers it. He doesn't speak a word; his face has drained of its entire color. I instinctively walk towards him, wanting to hold him, to comfort him and the closer I get, the clearer I can hear the screaming that is coming from an unknown source.

"But I didn't…"

He whispers so quietly that I can barely hear him.

"The judge decided this? But I didn't do it. I didn't steal anything."

There is no passion in his voice; he is already resigned to whatever is happening. I have honed in on the word 'judge' and I'm now trying to figure out what this could possibly mean. Surely judge means that this is somehow linked to the legal system…could it be a prison? What the hell am I in prison for? I must have been wrongly accused. Just like this boy! Maybe if we team up we can fight this system. How can I have committed a crime that I don't remember? With a newfound determination, I move over to the boy. I start to quickly and quietly tell him my plan, that we are both in here under false pretenses, but I can tell that he isn't listening. Doesn't he *want* to stand up for himself?

The crowd starts chanting louder and incoherently. A spotlight glares upon me and the boy. I start waving and yelling, begging for someone to listen to me, but I can barely hear myself over the racket, so I highly doubt that anyone else can. Someone comes up behind us and ushers us onto the running track. The boy comes to life, suddenly screaming, shouting and struggling. He really doesn't want to get onto this track!

"Come on I *work* here, you can't do that to me! I didn't steal anything I *didn't*…"

His pleas get no reaction.

"Knave you *know* once a judgment has been passed there isn't anything I can do. Sorry fella."

I do detect a note of sadness in the low, gruff voice which provides the very unhelpful answer. A panicky feeling rises up within me. Is there some sort of dictatorship going on in here? And what does he mean, he *works* here? I wish I could pull him to one side and get the answers I need, but I am placed very firmly on the starting line. I take in my surroundings, am I really supposed to race or something? This is mad. I want to argue, I want to kick up a fuss, they can't make me do this! But something about the conversation I overheard is making me nervous.

Sideshow

I feel like I need to just do as I'm told…for now at least.

I look over at three more people lined up alongside me. They also look panic-stricken, pale and desperate not to be standing where they are. I start to get the sensation that this race is going to be unexpected, to say the least. Every one of us jumps with a start when the announcement rings out loudly. I can't understand any of the words being spoken; it's as if it's in a different language. The cheering gets louder. I start to psyche myself up to run, unsure if it's something I am any good at. The gun blasts out and the three to my left take off quickly. As my feet start to move, I glance to my right and I witness a man with an old-fashioned style sword swiping the boy—Knave's—head clean from his shoulders.

Blood splatters everywhere and I try to stop to do something…anything. But my instinctive reaction is to keep running, to get as far away from the murderer as humanly possible. I try and organize my thoughts as I move, I try and get my brain to accept what just happened. I just saw a brutal killing. That poor boy who was falsely accused is now dead. Why? Is it because he was the slowest? Could I be next? This thought fills me with uncontrollable fear and I pick up the pace, now certain that this is a case of life and death. I don't want to die without even knowing who I am and why I'm being punished. That doesn't seem fair.

I seem to be moving very slowly, my limbs feel sluggish. I'm panting, unable to catch my breath. I glance up, trying to see how far behind I am when something trips me up. The crowd jeers as I fumble around; trying to see what caused my fall. I grab hold of a handful of hair and a horrible realization fills me up. It's another competitor, lay dead and mutilated at my feet. Someone has shredded her into pieces, even all of her fingers have been separated from her body. How did this happen in such a short time? I glance around wildly, screaming for help, desperate to be away from this awful situation. I don't want to do any of this anymore, whatever *this* is. Of course, no one can hear me and there is definitely no one coming to help.

Finally, I catch the eyes of someone in the audience. A very finely dressed woman. She is mouthing at me to run and I find my body complying. I know she's right, it's obvious, but that doesn't make it any easier. Everything in my body hurts, and this time I know for a fact that the wetness on my cheeks is tears. I don't want to carry on, however much I know I have to. Suddenly something knocks me sideways and the wind is taken right from me. A vibrating scream rips from my chest as if my body realizes what has hit me before my brain can connect. A head. A human head. One of the other runners. This is insane; it's like my worst nightmare. Surely the people running this show should be arrested. They are murdering people in cold blood, with no remorse.

My legs don't stop moving. There is a part of me, a very rational part that is keeping me going. It's the same, despicable part of me that keeps thinking that I only have one more person to beat. If I can win this, surely, I will be allowed to survive? That has *got* to be the point of this madness surely. An instinct kicks in; an adrenaline rush that I'm sure would allow me to outrun even the fastest athlete. Everything around me becomes a blur. Things hit into me, I have to dodge all sorts but I don't focus on anything, I don't concentrate on anything other than moving. Any distraction could kill me.

Suddenly someone pushes into me, forcing me off my path. The other competitor. I look up to see my fierce, determined expression mirrored in his. This is going to be harder than I first thought. Not only am I going to have to run fast, I'm going to have to sabotage my competitor. I'm going to have to sacrifice him, to condemn him to death. Can I do that? He certainly isn't bothered by my life.

I continue on, hoping to avoid any more confrontation so I won't be forced to let the darker, survival instinct that lies inside me, out. I don't really want to find out what sort of person I truly am. Soon I spot the finish line and I am spurred on towards the end. My heart is pumping furiously; my feet are pounding noisily against the ground. I want to win. I *need* to win. The boy is suddenly alongside me. We are neck and neck. I try and move sideways to avoid another shove, but end up losing valuable milliseconds of time. I need to do something and quickly. I take in a gulp of air. I need to do it, I *have* to. I close my eyes and push forwards; my hands reach out and I wait for the right moment. I connect with him, forcing him into the arms of a man holding a large shotgun.

The relief as I cross the line first is rapidly replaced with an all-consuming guilt as I hear the unmistakable gunshot go off. I don't look back, I don't need to. I already know that he's dead. I killed him. I effectively murdered someone. What have I become? I'm sure that I would like the person I was before, more than I like who I have seemed to become. If only I could *remember*. Even *one* good memory would help me right now.

I look down shaking my head, ignoring all of the excitement. Someone raises my arm above my head and places a plastic cup in my hands, but I don't move my eyes from my feet. I don't want to see anyone. I don't want to meet their judgmental eyes. As soon as they let go, I fall to the ground allowing myself to grieve. I may not know anyone here, that boy might have meant nothing to me, but it hurts so much. Deep in my chest. It's as much of a physical pain as it is a mental one.

I have been slumped over in the same position for such a long time that I don't even notice the silence that's surrounding me. I open my eyes tentatively and find myself in a desolate, corroding room. Gone are the people, the lights, and the twisted carnival décor. I am alone, on the cold, had a blank floor in a room that couldn't *possibly* be where I was running only moments before. There is no blood, no track, and no crowd. This place. This fucking hell hole has done it again! I want to wonder if I made it all up if somewhere in my deep, twisted, crazy mind I invented the whole thing. I want desperately to assume that this *is* a mental institution and that I am insane, but I know what I saw. I am certain of what happened.

Footsteps echo in the hall, but I don't move. In fact, after what I have done, I am willing to accept whatever is coming to me. I deserve it, but they just pass by me, as if I'm not even here. I look up to see an old man hunched over a brush. He starts whistling to himself, obviously working to clean up the room. I wonder if he knows what this place is and what just happened here. I don't ask, I have almost given up on wanting to know. Maybe I am better off ignorant. My voice speaks before I even decide to ask anything.

"Where is everyone?"

The gruff tone is still there, I sound shy, quiet and as if I have given up. Maybe I have. Maybe I should just lie here until someone comes along to kill me.

"I'm sure I don't know what you mean."

The pause lasts for a lifetime. I don't know what to say. I'm actually starting to doubt myself, the certainty from before is declining rapidly. How can someone who can't remember anything, be sure of what they've seen? Or felt? Or experienced at all? He leans in closer to me.

"That's Wonderland for you though."

The hushed tone doesn't go amiss. My heart leaps at this omission. Wonderland—what's that? The confusion must be evident in my features because he comes closer still until I can feel his breath in my ear.

"Come with me. I can't help you, but I know who can."

With this a whole new range of feelings run through me, one of them being positivity. I manage to muster up enough energy to stand on my feet, albeit a bit wobbly, to follow closely behind him discreetly. He is twitchy and very obviously nervous. He seems constantly certain that we're going to get caught because he keeps making me dart into doorways at every tiny sound. I can't even begin to imagine what his punishment would be for helping me. Horror runs through my mind before I can stop it. I am so terrified about this place; I'm not sure how much more I can take.

Finally, we enter a tiny room, where a young teenager is sat on a stool, chatting away on his mobile phone. He can't be much older than thirteen, he has black slicked-back hair and his jeans are slung low around his waist. I can't keep the disdain from my voice.

"*This?* This is the person who is going to tell me everything, to clear this whole nightmare up?!"

The young lad snaps his phone shut and stands up, placing his hands behind his back, trying to give off a superior air. I want to laugh at the absurdity of the situation. He makes this much worse by talking.

"Actually, I am a *lot* more important around here than I look—in fact, the place wouldn't be able to run without me. I'm the brains, the eyes, *and* the ears…"

I can sense that he is about to launch into a full rant and I turn to look desperately at the old man who brought me in, but he has already gone. Left without a sound or a trace. I dejectedly turn back, ready to have my ears chewed off by this idiot's self-importance, but instead, I am faced with a terrible sight. His intestines appear to be being pulled through his mouth by some sort of invisible force. He is gagging on the blood; his face is turning blue. His fingernails are so deep in the desk in front of him; he is leaving claw marks behind. I try to shout, but nothing comes out. I try to move, but my feet are frozen to the spot. I am completely and utterly unable to help. Again, I know someone is being killed and I am doing nothing to stop it. Instead, I squeeze my eyes shut, hoping to make it all disappear again, in the same way, that the running track did before, but when I nervously reopen one, the only thing that has changed is he is now lying dead on the floor. Stood on top of his lifeless body is a terribly fat, grinning man.

"Did…did you…?"

I don't finish my sentence, not really wanting to know any more details. I don't know how much more my stomach can take. I don't think I have ever seen death before, and suddenly I'm surrounded by it.

"Why?"

He lets out a booming, jovial laugh.

"Because he was an annoying twat!"

His laughter booms out again, echoing around the entire building. *He* doesn't seem frightened to be caught with me, but then again, he is obviously a terrifying man. He managed to kill someone without me even seeing him do it. Nerves start to kick in within myself, I know for a fact that he could kill me without batting an eyelid. I should run. I can probably outrun this guy, and if I get a head start by surprising him, I'm sure I'll be fine. Hopefully, he doesn't know this building inside and out because I'm certain I could lose him.

"Look, you were wasting your time with him. I'm the one who can tell you about Wonderland. I'm the only person who knows what is really going on here…Alice."

Alice.

I freeze. That's me, I'm Alice. Of course, I am, how could I have forgotten that? More memories flick through my mind, like a slideshow. Me as a young girl, sat covered in blood by my sobbing mother. Me as a teenager, partying and high on drugs. Me sat handcuffed in front of a police officer. The memories are all fuzzy and confusing, just like the others, but this time I'm *certain* that they're real, that they're mine. I don't know how I know this, I just do. I am disappointed by every single vision of myself. I have obviously not led a good life, a pleasing life. Somewhere along the line, I have gone wrong. They don't stop there. Then I see myself grinding up and down a cold silver pole, I see an unknown man handing me a wad of cash as I lie naked in a flea-bitten bed. I feel sick as I see the deadpan expression upon my face. Why am I doing all of these things? What sent me spiraling down such a seedy path? I don't want to believe it, I want to imagine that 'Wonderland' is somehow making me think these things, but they really resonate. I am feeling everything I see, I am experiencing these activities all over again.

"How do you know my name?"

I am angry at myself, for everything I'm seeing, for what I have done, but I redirect these emotions towards the fat man. He needs to take some of my wrath; it's his fault it all came flooding back after all. He laughs loudly, his eyes beadily watching my fists as they pump open and closed. I want out; whatever this is I want to get the hell away from here.

"Oh no, you couldn't *possibly* leave."

He drawls these words slowly, enjoying teasing me. I start to wonder if he can read my mind somehow.

"You haven't even got to the best part of the game yet!"

I take a sharp breath. Game? What does he mean by that? It seems I was wrong with all my ideas; it mustn't be a prison or a hospital. What sort of fucked up game murders people? This is the sickest thing I have ever been involved in. Come to think about it, how *did* I get involved? I let out a deep huff, trying to find some sort of positive in all of this. I suppose he didn't say I could *never* leave. Maybe if I complete this…game, I'll be allowed back out into the world. Although, from what I've seen of my life, do I *want* to be back out there? Maybe I can turn it all around. Maybe I can use this nightmare as a learning curve and I can somehow become a better person.

"Ok, so what's next?"

I try and muster up determination. I try and find a source of energy from somewhere. I can't imagine the next part is going to be easy. In fact, the race was probably the most pleasant part of all of this. To my surprise, the fat man has vanished, as if into thin air. Can he somehow turn invisible?

"God damn it, what is with all the crazy disappearing shit?"

Frustration bubbles up within me. Why is everything in here so bloody difficult? Surely it isn't essential to make it such a challenge. I start walking, unsure of what else I need to do, turning corners on a whim. With no directions, I have to just go where my instincts take me.

Finally, I hear voices. I peep into the room that they're coming from and am faced with a large banquet room. The smell of food is delicious and my stomach immediately starts rumbling reminding me that I haven't eaten for a very long time. My salivating mouth pushes me forward, hunger overcoming any other sensation. It isn't until I am fully inside the room that I notice three people sat at the table, drinking delicate cups of tea.

I try and assess them all, curious as to whether they are part of Wonderland, or contestants of the game, like me. Are they my competition? The man at the head of the table has a lopsided smile and a crazy outfit on. A tall hat sits on his head, decorated with stickers and badges. Braces stretch over his shoulders and attach to his multi-colored trousers, but underneath them is bare skin. Large scars run across his chest, making him look dangerous and also kind of sexy. I am weirdly attracted to him despite the fact that he is clearly a lot older than me. I am disgusted and intrigued by him in equal measures.

The smaller, frailer guy sat next to him seems frightened and twitchy. However strange he is coming across, I can relate to him. I feel exactly the same. His eyes keep flicking over to the first guy at the head of the table, suggesting to me that he is the leader of this little charade. The others must wait for his instructions. The third character in this scene is a small girl. She cannot be older than six. She is sat dozing over her drink, completely ignoring me. I watch her in fascination. What could this tiny innocent child be doing in this gory, sadistic hell? A tear pricks my eyes as I realize how messed up she must be. I am finding everything here difficult to take, so what must be going on in her head?

The next thing I am aware of is sitting at the table,

scoffing my face with cakes and cream tea. I don't know how I got to this position, did I black out for a while? Was I enslaved for a moment by my hunger? The three members of this tea party are laughing and joking around me, so I relax. Obviously, nothing sinister is going on here. Maybe this is just a lunch break or something. Suddenly a strange, soothing smell begins to infect my nostrils…

I open my eyes. Did I black out again? I glance around wildly; the entire room has changed again. Gone is the food and the long table, gone are the old-fashioned decorations. In their place is what I can only assume to be a bloody torture chamber. My heart rate increases as I see each new metallic instrument which I can only guess is there to cause me agony. I try to move, my hands are restricted, my ankles are tied up so tightly, I will never be able to get out of here. I gasp for air, panic racing through my veins, I can't do this. I don't want someone to do things to me whilst I have no control, that isn't fair. I can't beat this, there's no way I can win!

A gag is placed over my mouth by someone from behind me, taking away my last freedom. I can't scream, I can't shout, in fact, I can barely take in any air. This might be the thing to kill me. Maybe that'll be a blessing; at least I won't have to experience the terrifying torture. I don't even want to *imagine* what they will do to my corpse.

An unexpected blow comes from my left, racking through my whole body. I try to cough, I'm certain blood is already filling up in my mouth, but I'm prevented by the gag. Another from the right, across my ear. It's hot and sweaty; I see blood drip to the floor. The fear within me rises and falls, I want to do this, I *need* to do this, but a part of me wants to give up, to stop fighting and just let myself die. Death has to be more peaceful than this.

Sideshow

The punches continue. I have no idea how long for. It must be the men from the dining table; I wish I could see them to confirm this but all I can see is the blur around me as my head is forced from side to side. Finally, they come to a halt. Jubilation fills me, have I completed this test? Did I win, or whatever it is we do here? My head slumps forward, my body giving into the pain. My eyes want to sleep, but my brain is screaming at me to keep awareness about me at all times. This is the moment I have to decide; do I sink or swim? To I fight for my life of limply give up?

I slowly lift my head, vomit rising in my throat. I am regretting all of the food I consumed before. The little girl. She is stood right in front of me brandishing a sharp switchblade. I shake my head panicked. I try and silently communicate with her that this isn't right, that she doesn't need to do this. I want to tell her that this isn't a normal life, that I can help her, rescue her. But then I see the terrifying glint in her eye and it hits me. Her appearance is deceiving. She is the most evil of them all, the most horrifying person I will find in here. She's the leader, not any of the guys.

She walks over to a glass table which is full of all sorts of terrifying implements, without breaking eye contact once. She fingers each one carefully, examining each one with a smug, twisted smile plastered across her lips. I try and keep my face blank, I don't want her or anyone to figure out how frightened I really am, although my body betrays me and sweat drips into my eyes. She gets slower with each one, and I just know that she is going to pick something soon, and I won't be able to stop her from doing anything she likes to me.

Suddenly a deafening crash shatters the tension in the room and all the torture weapons clatter to the ground.

Sideshow

The girl has smashed the glass using only one of her tiny hands. She picks up a shard and brings it to me, gliding it gently up and down my arm. The piece is so jagged that even this light movement splits my skin and warm blood trickles to my fingertips. I try and cry out in pain, but this just restricts my airwaves further. The pressure becomes more intense and my heart is thumping hard in my chest. The vomit in my throat swirls around and threatens to spill out more with each movement. As the glass works its way up my inner thigh, a dizzy spell takes me. I try and keep my eyes open, I can't pass out now, not with what she is about to do to me. She is going to ruin me forever; she is going to completely destroy my body. But I can't...they close...my mind wanders...

Cold water splashes across my face, making me awaken with a start. A scream rises out of my chest and I am startled to hear it out loud. I'm am gag free. The pain has also dulled; it is now more of a steady throb as if the brutal events happened hours before. A tut from behind me makes me jump and I start to thrash, I can't take any more. I don't want to see those three ever again. I don't think I will ever know what they did to me while I blacked out, but I can stop them now.

To my relief, the face that comes before me is not one of the three sick bastards from the table, but the lady who convinced me to keep going in the race. The one who mouthed at me to run. My body sags with relief. I don't know this woman, she is clearly something to do with this place, but for some reason, I feel like I can trust her. I think it's her kind eyes. Plus, the fact that she is gently wiping the dried matted blood from my skin. She is whispering under her breath and I try and make out some of her words.

"It's a good job I stopped them when I did…who knows…too far sometimes!"

I want to speak out to her, but I think I'm still in shock. I don't understand her actions at all, she is the only person in this entire hell hole who has been openly nice to me and to be honest, I don't know how to react to it. Sure, the fat man explained things to me, but I would no way describe his actions as 'nice'. A small part in my brain is warning me that this is the woman I should be most afraid of, that the nicest people are always the ones to watch out for, but I push this to one side. I don't need any more negativity at this point.

"Alice? Alice are you with me?"

I suddenly realize that she is now openly addressing me. I try and nod my head, but the movement is stiff, jerky and hurts like hell.

"I'm Duchess…well, I'm actually Dora but no one has called me that for years. Are you ok? Can you walk? I'll help you, come on lean on me."

I try and get my balance as she grips tightly onto my arms. My brain is swimming, my vision fuzzy. Her touch is ice cold against my skin and I try and figure out in my addled state what that means. I can't connect my brain with my voice box, so instead, I try to focus on her words.

"Duchess!"

A loud, booming voice breaks through my shock barrier and sets my heart racing all over again. We both spin around and are faced with the fat man. He only has to look at Duchess to have her nervously shuffling off. Is he in charge or something? I watch her go sadness filling me up. I don't know what it is about her, but when she was near, I felt lighter. Maybe she was just another part of the weirdness that makes up Wonderland. The only place on

Earth that seems to have no logic.

I am roughly pulled along by the fat man and I watch the grin that never seems to leave his face. What has he got to be so happy about? Does he get a sick joy from hurting others? I want to stop; I don't want him to take me on to some other challenge or game. I'm still far too battered and bruised. I wonder what these 'events' are supposed to prove? Speed? Durability? Strength? If so, I have simply got through by luck. I don't want to risk anymore. My mind won't be able to take it.

I am thrown into a room and my body crashes against the floor. A weep emanates from me before I can reign myself in. I just feel sorry for myself now. I don't know how I ended up here and it just seems downright cruel. I start to look around me, to see what horrors I am going to be faced with next. To my surprise, I see five other people, all in very similar beaten up conditions to me, all with the same petrified expressions. These must be the other competitors. I don't recognize any of them so maybe we are the final five. Maybe this hell is almost over. Maybe I am about to find out the truth.

I force myself to my feet and look closer at my competition. Three girls are sat on chairs in the corner, each one looking at their feet. I can tell instantly that I won't have any trouble from these. They have been through too much, probably worse than what I have. They have given up; there isn't a spark of hope in any of their eyes, just fear. I can almost feel their experiences running through me, and I can see that I have received the better end of the deal. At least I haven't been forced into sexual shame.

A tall boy is standing near a set of shelves containing books. When he sees me watching him, he picks one up and starts to comment on it loudly. His grammar is confusing; he keeps using long, complex words that don't fit in with his sentences. He is quite clearly a pompous twat. I'll have no problem defeating him. I almost want to do it here and now so I don't have to listen to his waffle anymore.

The last boy, who is hunched in the corner, is eyeing me incredibly suspiciously, more so than just as competition. His emotions seem to run deeper than that. I give him a perplexed look back, what could I have possibly done to have him mistrust me? He doesn't even know me?

Or does he?

Something about him is incredibly familiar. I instinctively step closer towards him and as I do another flash of memory hits me hard. This boy is stood with his arms around a girl, kissing and hugging playfully. In the next scene, she is dead, her limbs removed from her body. I gasp audibly, did he kill his girlfriend? Is that why he's here? How could I *possibly* know that? I rapidly move back, not wanting to see any more.

A curtain at the end of the room starts to lift, and the others all move into a line formation. I do the same, joining on at the end, unsure of what else to do. The girl stood next to me is visibly trembling and her fear just makes me more nervous. I see through the crack that a crowd has gathered. I wonder why there was no audience for only the second part of my journey.

The noise is deafening, I hold my hands over my ears to protect my eardrums, but soon realize that this could be part of the challenge, and so hastily let them drop. I can't show weakness. The fat man is stood at a podium, talking to the audience. It is obvious from this that he is some sort of games master. I guess I suspected as much. He didn't want to help me; he just wanted to keep the whole operation running smoothly. Big letters light up with the word 'Wonderland' and I feel sick to my stomach as people cheer along.

We are all introduced and discussed in a blur. I can't remember any of it; I can't focus on a single sound. Until the 'final challenge' is announced. We are all handed a selection of weapons; guns, knives, swords, and told to fight to the death. I actually laugh out loud at this. Do they really expect us to do this? Do they really think that we are going to kill each other for their entertainment? I refuse to go into it, *knowing* that the aim is death.

The claxon sounds and I cross my arms over my chest, making a stand. Determination is fixed on my face. Unfortunately, none of the others seems to feel the same way as me. The whole thing is a bloodbath. I scream as the pompous boy lands, dismembered at my feet. I see limbs flying, gunshots ring out and knives slash through the air. I drop everything, except a katana. I grip onto the handle tightly, feeling my face go deathly pale. I tell myself that I am only going to defend myself, that I have caused enough death without administered it in a brutal way myself.

Before I have even moved my feet, the three girls have also been taken out. I don't want to look at the chaos that lies on the floor. I keep my eyes fixed on the last remaining survivor. The one that I recognized. Jeers rise up from the crowd, but I don't react. He stands still too, smirking at me wildly. The commentator is stunned into silence, obviously not expecting us to stand there, vulnerable and still. Soon he starts to try and provoke us. I ignore it all and try to work out *how* I know this boy. He is waiting for me to figure it out, I just know it. Nothing else comes, just the same memory from before. Suddenly a voice from the crowd brings it all flooding back.

"Come on Alice, this dickhead killed your sister!"

I fall to the floor as the images come in thick and fast. My sister, my beautiful loving sister, who had such a better quality of life than me. He was her boyfriend; they were together for many, many years. He wasn't good to her. He was a controlling cheat, but she wouldn't listen to reason. She loved him with all of her heart. Until the day she found him in bed with me. He was paying me of course, I wouldn't have done it if I didn't need my fix so badly...I tried to argue that with her, but of course she didn't want to know. She didn't care that it was all for drugs, it was a betrayal, pure and simple. The argument got out of hand, so out of hand that he killed her. Stabbed her just once through the heart. Then he proceeded to try and get me involved with the body removal, but I was too scared, too sad. He cut her into pieces and buried her in the woods. My sister, the beautiful, intelligent Lorina.

I stand up, my matted hair falling in front of my eyes. Everyone cheers. I don't feel like myself anymore, I feel like a monster has risen up inside of me. One that wants revenge, one that wants to avenge my sister, to make up for all the shitty things I've done. Especially to her. I lift the katana up and push it towards him. He laughs and does a stupid victory-style dance. He is showing off, gaining the audience's approval. He is putting on a display because he doesn't think I have got it in me. Maybe we have been here before, who knows? I hold it over his chest and force it lightly. The smile is wiped clean from his face. His whole demeanor and attitude changes, he starts begging and backing away. Soon he is up against the wall and I can drive it in through his heart. I do so slowly and with immense force. I enjoy the blood splattering across my face; I love this feeling of power, the sensation that I am finally doing something right. As his life ebbs away, the cheers get louder. Soon he slumps dead on the ground. It is a hollow victory. No one has really won. I am still bad. I'll never be able to make up for that.

A jolly man with a nametag that reads 'King' pushes a plastic crown on my head. The obviously supposed to be some sort of joke. Whoever he is, the crowd loves him. They are lapping up every single one of his words. Flowers are shoved into my arms and a medal hung around my neck. I don't smile even once. I've won and now I want to go. I've been forced to do things that I already bitterly regret; I don't need any sort of recognition. Camera's flash in my face and I also notice that I'm being videoed. This entire thing is probably televised in some sort of sick reality show. A terrifying woman, in a long regal gown, lets out a cackle which silences the room.

"Now for your prize Alice."

She ignores me as I shake my head. I don't want anything, why would I after everything I've suffered? I am alive and that's enough. I have already lost my humanity, my dignity and everything that makes me a decent person. Of course, what I want doesn't matter; it's all about the entertainment. A large screen appears above my head and displays a video close up of my face. It's the version of me that I've seen in my memories; the druggie, the criminal, the shambles of a woman. I am sat nervously in a seat and someone encourages me to talk. I feel a weird nervous anticipation at what I am about to see.

"Hi…I'm Alice Pleasance. I…um…I want to apply to be a contestant on Wonderland."

I watch, stunned. I chose this? I actually *wanted* to do this? On the screen, I raise my head.

"I *need* to do this; my life has gone to crap. I've gone to prison for a crime that wasn't my fault. I'm on death row…what else could I possibly have to lose? *None* of this was my fault. There are people who did this to me. It's their fault I'm this way."

I'm confused, is the crime my sister's murder? I can't have done anything worse surely? And who are all these people I'm blaming for my behavior? I'm the one to blame for my actions, of course, I am. I might not like that, but it's the truth. A mystery voice then interrupts me on screen.

"Can you please tell me what your understanding of Wonderland is? We need to be *certain* that every contestant is fully aware of what they're committing to."

I watch my eyes flicker from side to side, an odd emotion on my face. I'm stunned as I see myself taking in a deep breath, preparing myself for my next sentence.

"Wonderland is where you go to win your chance at revenge. It's designed for people like me, people that are going to die anyway. There are casualties, but that's just the sacrifice needed to be made for television entertainment. That's the only thing people want to watch anymore. Once you are in, you don't leave. I've watched it enough to understand the challenges. Each game will be a risk of my life, but if I get through it all, the risk will have been worth it."

I feel sick. I came here, *knowing* I would never leave? Wouldn't prison have been a kinder end to my shitty life?

"I spend my entire childhood being bullied by the same group of people. They're the ones that I want revenge on. They destroyed my self-worth; they *literally* took away my chance to develop a personality. I was beaten mentally and physically for years. Without them, I could have been normal, I could have made something of myself…I could have been more like my sister. I turned to drugs when I was still young, to escape the pain. This led onto other things…terrible things. I'm sure you all know the story. I have done some bad things, but I'm *not* a bad person. Not deep down. I want to prove that."

I watch the tears fill my eyes. I see the desperation, but I still can't understand my decision. Maybe I just didn't fully comprehend in my drug-addled grieving mind.

"But if I do this, if I get to exercise my demons, do to them what they did to me, I can be cured or all of my issues. I just know it. I can't die without doing *something*, without standing up for bullied children all over the world. I *know* others will understand my plight."

I'm holding my breath, clearly resonating with everything that I'm saying. I've been to hell and back in my life, but I'm still shocked that it brought me here.

"Just to be clear; your memories will be cleared on a daily basis to ensure no competitor has an advantage and you will be thrown into situations where it is kill or be killed. The producers *want* your humanity stripped away by the end of each day. They *want* a good show. They don't want you to back out of the murders at the end of the program, that's the part people like best."

I glance around wildly as the screen descends into darkness, trying to figure out what this last statement means. Is it not over? Do I have to kill someone else now? But…who? There isn't anyone left. Finally, my eyes connect with the terrifying lady who has taken over the running of the show. She gives me a wide, suggestive toothless grin which sends chills up and down my spine.

"Well, Alice…"

Sideshow

Her long drawn out sentence is weighted with expectation. Whatever it is they want me to do now I'll refuse. I'm done; I've already done too much for them.

"You must be very pleased. You are the only contestant to have survived this long. You have killed almost all your chosen revenge targets, in fact, this will be your sixth and last. There has been a lot of talk about what to do with you...after. Obviously, you can't keep playing, and we *certainly* can't set you free!"

Everyone laughs as my heart sinks down to the ground. I was just given a tiny glimmer of hope, before having it stripped away again in the same sentence.

"So instead, we have decided to offer you a job here. You can come and work at Wonderland, isn't that fantastic! Now, to the bit everyone has been waiting for..."

A screen pulls back to reveal a girl who is tied up in a ridiculous amount of restraints. She is trying to struggle and scream but to no avail. Melissa. The worst bully of them all, the ringleader of the group who made my life a living hell. A flash of hatred burns in my chest then fizzles out as quickly as it came. Another video starts up showing all of my previous five victims and I can't help but stare, unable to avoid the horror developing in front of me. I wince at the brutality of each of the murders I committed. The loathing is evident in my body language and expression. Did any of them *really* deserve that? Sure, they gave me a bad time, but *I* messed up my life, not them. No one should be killed for the amusement of others. Why did I agree to any of this?

The katana is handed to me, it is obviously my favorite weapon, and I turn to face Melissa. If I just do this, if I kill just *one* more person I won't have to play anymore. I'll be allowed to live, sure I'll have to work here, but it might be easier to deal with from the other side. I already have a friend in Duchess. I have already killed so many; one more won't hurt, will it? Melissa is such a bitch, maybe I *should* do it for bullied victims? I want to laugh at the fear in her eyes. What a role reversal.

I hold the katana out in front of me and slowly start to walk. Melissa whimpers and I laugh loudly. The crowd stays silent as I pierce skin with the sword. A loud gasp fills the air as blood trickles down. I am calm and considered with my actions, no more being ruled by my emotions. I want this death to be simplistic, not just for show. I smile at the girl who was always awful to me as everything slips away. Relief floods through me when I realize it's done, I'm free from this game. My body slumps to the ground, and as the blood gushes out, so does my soul. I have saved someone; I have finally done something right. I am leaving Wonderland, in fact, I'm leaving this Earth, but on my own terms. That is something to be proud of.

Even if nothing else is.

The Freak
Kevin Hall

It was born with a genetic mutation. Its face was sunken, and it had large dark holes for eyes, with the pupils small, sharp and staring in the center. A long, stretched out mouth and flat nose, with rows of sharp, black teeth and a round body. Its hands had three fingers on each, with stubby legs.

Yet Margery loved it dearly, convinced it was a boy, and she would bring her son up in a world where he would be loved and not feared or hated. Alas, this was not meant to be. She would be pointed at and ridiculed for years, and many attempts were made to end her life and her child's. She would end up coming to regret it, hate it, and then immediately regret she had even thought that.

Margery tried her best to raise her son like any other, but even at an early age, he was not behaving like a normal human being would. He would have temper tantrums every hour, wailing like nothing she had heard before, screaming and stamping about, breaking things around the house when she wasn't looking…and actually laughing about it.

Of course, Margery put this down to terrible behavior, but when he continued to do it at four and five, enough was enough. She had tried to take him out in public; to show the world that she cared for him no matter what he looked like, but people would shriek in fear, cower away and even throw things at her and him. At one point someone even threw a brick with glass shards stuck on it at her direction.

Counseling and psychiatrists could do nothing, with some even commenting that he was an abomination and should have been destroyed at birth. He was the freak of the town that she couldn't even take him to a proper school, so she tried to educate him herself.

Margery's world was falling around her, and there was nothing she could do about it...or at least until the stranger came calling. He was tall, much taller than any human being Margery had seen and had to stoop to get through her front door. He was also very thin and had long, spindly fingers and sharp, black nails, as he held out a hand to shake hers. His face was partially obscured with a large bowler hat. He simply called himself Six, and that he had two other brothers who would all care for the child. His lower part of the face was grey and shriveled and stunk of decades worth of shit, and when he grinned he had black, sharp teeth.

Margery was beside herself at this point and would do anything anyone said, and when she signed on the parchment she had no idea—until much later when it was too late—what she had done. "Anything...anything to make the disease go away. I just want a normal child and one who is loved."

Six placed a very cold hand onto Margery's warm shoulder and led her to the couch. His voice sounded like when someone scrapes their nails along a blackboard; cold, raspy and ancient. "Do not worry about the boy, Margery. He is in safe hands and will be returned to you good as new. Now that we have your contract and compliance, the ritual will take place in the next day or so. You may feel some levels of discomfort, but that is to be expected. We will return then."

Margery watched as Six led the boy—head concealed with a blanket—out her front door and into a long, black car, with red front headlamps and blacked out windows. She could have sworn she heard the car growl as it drove away, but maybe it was her imagination.

666

The first symptoms appeared just an hour after Six had left. Margery began to violently throw up and even dark blood came out. Her stomach hurt like hell, and as she sat there at the edge of the toilet, blood streaming the loo and walls, a pounding headache started. What had she signed up to? She hadn't even had time to read the small print. Margery went to take two of the strongest painkillers she could find and a glass of water. She decided to clean up the mess and take a bath.

As she relaxed in the bubbles and warm water, Margery started to feel a little better. Maybe what Six had planned for her son would cure him, make him a better person for it. She certainly prayed and hoped so. Before she knew it, Margery had drifted off into an uneasy sleep.

She awoke with a start a few moments later, after a pulling sensation on her lower back was causing her to slip into the water. It was tugging her down and Margery had to thrash at the sides and grip them to stop herself from drowning. In a panicked state, and with all her might, she pulled away from the force and felt a rip and squelch, then a searing pain.

Margery clambered out of the bath, shivering and wincing, letting the water slip away down the drain…along with dark blood and a large brown clump of flesh she hadn't seen before. She dared to place her hand on her lower back, and felt a long, slimy…a tail? No, this cannot be.

Margery composed herself and went to the mirror. Indeed, there was half a tail on her back, swaying slightly, brown and sticky, the bottom of it a clump of blood after she had yanked some of it off down the drain. She must be a hallucination, brought on by the stress and heartache of recent weeks. A dry down, loungewear and a glass of wine should ease things a bit.

After taking more painkillers, Margery settled down on the sofa with a book and a drink and began to feel a little better. It was then that she felt a massive swelling on her face and her a searing pain through the right side of her mouth. She dropped her wine, the glass shattering and the wine staining the dark green carpet. The bulge on her right chin was growing and stretching at an astonishing rate.

In a state of panic, Margery went to the kitchen and reached for a large carving knife. She went to the hall mirror to take a closer look. She staggered back at her sight. The right side of her face was completely sunk in and shriveled, her right eye baggy, black and hollow, except for a small white dot for a pupil, that stared hideously back at her. A large blot had formed below this, and it looked to be alive, pulsating with blue and red veins.

Margery screamed and began slicing away at it with her knife, blood gushing to the floor and spraying the mirror. But no matter how many times the knife struck, the blot would grow back and seemed to be bigger than before. Margery collapsed to the floor and ruffled a hand through her hair. Clumps started to fall out too. What the hell was happening to her?

Her tired mind couldn't comprehend what was going on, but before she knew it, she had sunk into a deep sleep.

666

Margery had no idea how long it had been since she had been there, but she awoke to the sound of knocking at her door and still searing pain from her mouth. She tried to speak but no sound would come, her throat felt very dry and sore. She got up slowly and painfully, before edging towards the front door.

But before she could turn the handle, a letter fell through her door, and she gingerly took it, opening it up.

Dear Mrs. Brundle,

I trust by now you are starting to turn. Your son is well on the way to recovery, sorry it took slightly longer than we first thought. My brothers, Six and Six, were able to remove the monstrosity parts you so hated and make him…partly human again. However, there seems to be some murderous intentions in him that we are trying to control. You will see him before your time is up, so don't worry—at least there is progress!

I am sorry this letter took five years to reach you, but these things take time. The transformation effects will take hold a lot faster now. Thank you for your patience. I will be in touch soon.

Yours, Six.

Margery shook her head at the last paragraph. No…that must be a spelling error. Surely Six meant five HOURS and not YEARS. She looked at her watch. Instead of October 1st, 2018, it read October 2nd, 2023.

No…

There was another push of her letterbox, and a glass tablet came through, showing a digitized version of the local newspaper. The front photo was actually moving, and Margery could see the headline that sent shivers down her spine.

FREAK OUT –
WAR AGAINST HUMANS BEGINS
FREAKS STRIKE BACK

She shivered again as she saw her name in the article. Apparently, she had outraged other people with deformities and they wanted her head. She had started the third World War and many humans had already lost their lives. No, no, no, this was not happening to her. She deserved better!

There was a lot of commotion outside her house, and Margery still heard loud banging and shouting coming from outside. The door suddenly burst open and splintered, and about six Freaks of various deformities came in, shouting and swearing, carrying knives, chainsaws, and pickaxes, who all descended on Margery, slicing away at her…

Margery woke with a start, still at the mirror. Jesus, it had just been a dream after all. But her abnormality was still apparent. She could feel her tail and the swollen blot had gotten bigger. Margery decided it was high time to look at the copy of the parchment she had been given.

Getting up, she made her way to the kitchen and picked up the scroll. At the bottom was the fine print—which many people don't bother reading, and in her tired mind, she didn't read it.

Sideshow

PS: I want to personally thank you for being a part of this little experiment. To take your son's Freak deformities and make them a part of you, is a truly generous and human act. You shall have probably more symptoms than he does, and will suffer pain, to begin with, but you will come to live with it. The Dark Ones thank you also for your kind contribution and a special place in the Dark awaits you once this is all over. I trust by now you are feeling some of the transformations take effect. Do not worry. Your boy will be returned soon.

Six.

Margery began to see it was making sense now. She had given herself over to evil, who wanted to make her a Freak and teach her a lesson for not loving her son for who he was. She got it and was ready to accept it. She just needed her son back in her life, to tell him she was sorry and for just to be who he was.

It was then that there was a knock at the door. Margery got up and moved slowly towards it. Her hands were beginning to shrivel and turn grey. Her mouth was now full of small, sharp teeth. Most of her hair had fallen out and her face was now sunken, both eyes black holes with staring, white small pupils.

The door opened a Six stood there with his two brothers. "Aah, Mrs. Brundle. I see the changes have moved along more quickly than we first thought. Please do not worry about your son. He has been cured and is with a foster family now, who will love him more than you could. Please, come with us. It is time to join the Dark Order."

Six handed her a hat which covered her face apart from her mouth.

"I see it now," Margery croaked. "I see the darkness. But I also see we can change people's fate. No matter the cost."

Six grinned. "Good, good, Mrs. Brundle. We have much to discuss but so little time. The Freak War will soon be upon us. Come. Nightmarish things await."

With that, Margery left her house, never to return again.

Kevin Hall

Kevin Hall is a writer of horror short stories - Thirteen Vol. 1 and Thirteen Vol. 2: The Horror Continues are a collection of self-published short stories available on amazon. He is currently writing Vol.3: The Never-Ending Nightmare, with Vol. 4: Vengeful Ghosts sub-missions now open. He is also in the middle of writing his first novel- Ravens Edge, a supernatural horror set in a small Scottish town, and is also writing several 2000AD scripts and a Bride Of Candy-man film script. He is a keen Nintendo gamer, loves going to the cinema and musicals, and is a big fan of Katy Perry and Stephen King. Kevin's goal is to become a full-time writer and hopefully, the next Stephen King.

Clown in the Mirror
Katie Jaarsveld

Dedicated to all those who dislike clowns or have been scared witless by them.
My sons, Nicholas and Dustin, being two of them.

Intro

The fear of clowns is coulrophobia.

The history of clowns is conflicting. When you search for their history, each site dictates a different timeline.

Clowns were a form of amusement throughout history, by various names. Harlequin, King's Fool, Court Jester, Mr. Punch, and many more.

From Egypt to China in the Zhou Dynasty, Ancient Greece, Ancient Rome, over a huge span in time and cultures.

Then someone decided to use clowns to scare. No more Mr. Nice Clowns for laughs. Turnabout is fair play.

Sideshow

Chapter 1

You saw that, didn't you? A light flashed on a clown's face and you saw a gruesome face with fangs and red, glowing eyes.

The light turned on and then you saw a smiling clown with smeared greasepaint, smelling of stale cigarette smoke and making animal shapes from balloons. There were always balloons.

My first time at the circus was both thrilling and terrifying. A clown went into the Hall of Mirrors and what I saw in each mirror was not the reflection of the clown who had entered before me. Each face was more gruesome than the one before.

His faces should have made me feel terrified. Instead, they thrilled me.

I wanted to know how he changed his face in the mirrors and I wanted to be able to do it with my own face as well.

At an early age, clowns became my obsession. The clothes, shoes, the designs on their faces formed in greasepaint.

Their unique traits and capabilities, their many talents. The acts, no matter how silly, individual or in a group.

I wanted to be a clown. Instead, I would become a doctor.

My parents had indulged my going to every carnival I wanted to go to, as long as it didn't interfere with my studies, and my room stayed clean.

My test scores soared with straight A's, my room was immaculate with everything having its own place. I even left my bedroom door open, so my parents could see it was *that* clean.

Sideshow

What they never looked in, or noticed, was the trunk in the bottom of my wardrobe. I thought they assumed it was toys, hobby stuff, winter clothes or blankets, whatever people used trunks for.

My trunk held my dreams and my clown paraphernalia. I saved my allowance from my chores to purchase my dream items. Costumes, different grease-paints, noses, and gimmick items like balls to juggle, balloons with a pump. After a time, I started saving my money for bigger items. I concentrated on sketches of faces and tried different combinations to make my face.

I was given a Polaroid camera with film for my birthday, so I could even take pictures of my faces in the mirror if I wanted. I took pictures of the family at the carnival, with clowns always in the background.

While I loved my parents and our dog, I wanted to see the clowns faces, and to see if they changed on camera as they did in the Hall of Mirrors. They didn't.

Sideshow

Chapter 2

As I grew older, I formulated a plan. What career path could I take which would allow me to maximize my love of clowns? A doctor, or rather a plastic surgeon. I could feed the vanity of people while honing my skills for the ultimate change in faces.

With my having made straight A's, a scholarship was easy. My parents were pleased with my progress. With both of them being doctors, my Mom a surgeon and Dad a heart specialist, they were impressed with my career choice. They even bought me a studio apartment in a gated community, which was close to the clinic I had planned to intern with.

The apartment would need minor renovations and a coat of paint. Everything was white. They hired guys to do the work and move me in. My beloved trunk was on the first load to my apartment. Mom offered to have it refinished or purchase a new one, but this was my dream trunk and my dreams would stay intact.

They had tried to purchase everything I looked at from a catalog, for my apartment. Even when I really didn't want an item. As a result, I had very little furniture in my apartment. A chair, bed, night stand with a boring lamp. No color but that could be changed.

I did, however, let them purchase some frames. I wanted to blow up a couple of photos and place them on the mantle. You know, to show the love of my family and for clowns.

They knew I loved clowns, maybe they just hadn't realized the extent.

I had continued going to carnivals until I was supposed to start my clinical rotation in college. I was saddened that

Sideshow

I wouldn't be able to attend regularly, as I had over the years. A few of the performers and clowns knew me by name since I had been such a regular.

This would be my last attendance for a while, so I had been looking forward to going that night. While I was eating in the common room for the apartments, I saw an ad for a multiplex. There were posters and billboard signs advertising horror movies, one, in particular, was a clown.

I was outraged. How dare they diminish the importance of clowns by making them the ultimate evil. Kids with their parents were walking past me, the kids crying when they saw the clowns. Why? Clowns were loved. Now, these kids were crying and having tantrums to not enter the theater? Kids being threatened to *be good, or the clowns will get you.* By their parents.

Kids were supposed to be afraid of the monster under the bed or in the closet, not clowns.

I couldn't get away from them fast enough. As soon as I walked into my apartment, I picked up photos of the clowns. My beloved clowns, now the source of ridicule and hatred. I pondered on what I would do as I set the frames back in their places.

I sat down and contemplated the scene I had just witnessed. If they wanted to be afraid of clowns, maybe they needed a reason. Maybe parents needed to be afraid, not the children.

I went to my trunk and opened it, gently unwrapping the fabric from the tissue I had stored it in. My costumes. I slid my hands over the material with a lover's hand, caressing the fabric.

Placing it back in the tissue, I opened the cosmetic box with the greasepaint and inhaled. The smell was the best smell I knew of. It made me lightheaded and giddy with joy.

I would be seeing clowns tonight. I placed everything back in its place in the trunk. Closing it, I ran my hand over the lid of the trunk. My dreams.

It was time to get ready for the carnival. A knock on my door and a lady came in with candy. After I swallowed it, I became sleepy and lay down, staring at my photos.

Sideshow

Chapter 3

I always wore muted tones to the carnival. I didn't want to take away from the colors of the clowns or the performers. However, my underclothes and socks were statement pieces to how much I loved the clowns.

I always chose vibrant colored socks, as it was easy access. Socks with clowns, faces, ducks, everything you could imagine were printed on socks. They were so soft, they made me think of the sweet softness of my costume. And it made me hungry. I needed to touch the softness. It took me to a happy place. I could smile and touch a sock, then my heart would start beating faster, I would start breathing harder. I was excited.

Then I remembered the kids crying. My happy place was shattered, and the excitement diminished. I was angry. I would talk with the clowns and see what they felt, where their happy place was. What they looked like without makeup, if they even took it off.

At the carnival, I showed my season pass and greeted the clown in the booth. He waved me through and continued working with the customers in the line behind me.

I strode over to the tent where clowns were standing outside. It was off-limits to the public, but they knew and liked me, so it was all good.

Beep-beep was my favorite. He didn't actually speak in costume, just honked his nose or said *meep meep*. He was cool. Every interaction, I understood. There was a language there which many would not have understood. I did.

Sideshow

I mentioned the clown movie, and many laughed it off. A few like Bopper looked sad. However, Beep-beep and Chip looked furious.

I asked Beep-beep and Chip if they ever took their makeup off. Both immediately shook their heads no and looked appalled that I had asked. I told them my profession and they were interested.

Beep-beep's makeup looked normal clownish until you looked deep. There were scars underneath. Cutting scars and cigarette burns.

Beep-beep pointed them out, not breaking character. He opened his mouth, and his tongue was half missing. He shrugged his shoulders and looked at Chip.

Chip stated outright that his skin was not in good shape and the makeup hid the teen marks damaging him. He explained Beep-beep was born with a defection in his mouth, so he escaped the ridicule and punishments by being who he became.

Beep-beep nodded furiously and meeped.

Then *he* walked in.

Chapter 4

I knew his face right off. He was the one from my childhood, the one whose face changed in the Hall of Mirrors. He looked exactly the same.

He walked up to me and stared, taking my face in his hand by my chin. He turned my face this way and that looked me all around. "He'll do." He walked off.

Chip's mouth dropped open, as did Beep-beep's. I pushed up at Chip's chin to close his mouth. He did the same to Beep-beep.

"Man, he never speaks. He is the ultimate loner. How the hell do you know Jack and why?" Chip sounded astonished and as though he admired me at the same time.

I recanted my brief meeting with him in the Hall of Mirrors, however, I hadn't been aware he had seen me. Did he recognize me? Had he even noticed me?

The Hall of Mirrors was a maze of puzzles with distorting mirrors as obstacles with glass panes keeping the visitors from parts they did not have access to. Some mirrors were concave, the mirror being curved outward, making the subject to appear short and fat. Some mirrors were convex, the mirror being curved inward, making the subject to appear tall and thin.

I didn't remember either of us changing shape, only his face changing its appearance. As a boy, I was taller than most children, and this clown towered me by a good 28 cm.

While I didn't know what he thought I'd do, I wanted desperately to know how Jack changed his face in the mirrors. The only way I would find out would be to follow him.

Sideshow

As I had walked through the tents, I saw a Hall of Mirrors. I didn't know there were still any in circulation. I was getting excited. This had to be where Jack went.

I felt goosebumps on my neck and arms as I entered the Hall. I smelled something pungent, like rotting soil. It got stronger the further I went in.

There was a chair surrounded by the mirrors and he was sitting there as if he knew I was coming.

"So, you've come home." his voice was a deep croak that had a familiar sound to it, which I couldn't place.

He reached into a trunk by the chair and produced a shard of mirror. He threw it to me. I surprised myself by catching it. I looked at the shard in my hand. It felt familiar and welcoming.

Sideshow

Chapter 5

Jack was laughing. The room was spinning. I knew this rabbit hole and welcomed it. As I fell, I remembered.

I had cut his face with shards of mirror. With every slice I made, his face changed in a mirror. I had made him a permanent clown.

I heard yelling and it had felt as if I was being dragged. There were sirens and people talking to me whom I couldn't identify.

When I came to, a bright light was over my head and I felt funny, not in a laughing way.

I had tried sitting up, only to find I was tied to the bed. I had started laughing then I felt a stick. I had been given a shot.

I next woke up hearing two men talk about mirrors. I closed my eyes and listened. I wanted to know about the mirrors.

"The carnival manager didn't know where the Hall came from. It had been destroyed years ago after that freak cut himself up in there. He kept yelling he was a clown now."

"Didn't this guy say the same thing?"

I could feel them looking at me. I opened my eyes quickly and they both jumped. I smiled but it felt like I was already smiling.

A doctor came in and asked how I was feeling. He had reached down to touch my face, but I didn't feel anything, so maybe he wasn't touching me.

He took bandages off my face. Had I been hurt by the clown? The doctor was shaking his head. The guards gasped, and the nurse ran out of the room with her hand over her mouth.

Sideshow

"I tried to repair the damage to your face, but even with my skills, you would still look different. There are simply too many scars and cuts.

I asked for a mirror and the doctor sent for one. The nurse came back in with a mirror, but she wouldn't make eye contact.

A guard had been given instruction to untie one of my wrists. I took the mirror and stared into it.

I recognized this face. There were new cuts, but Jack was looking at me in the mirror. I started laughing. I realized what I had forgotten long ago. *I was Jack.*

It was me I was cutting in the Hall of Mirrors all those years ago. I wasn't a plastic surgeon, I had plastic surgery to *repair my face* from the damage I had caused. I had wanted to be a clown so much that I had carved one in my face.

I looked around my room and saw Beep-beep and Chip in the photos. They waved at me. I heard a *meep meep* and I smiled.

The guards untied my other arm and I sat up in bed. I was staring at the photos while the guards were talking to the doctor.

"You know they closed the Hall of Mirrors, right? I heard that they dismantled it and were going to melt down the mirrors."

"Creepy place if you ask me. I never did like them. Or clowns."

At that, I looked at them and smiled the best smile I could give them.

I knew three truths if I knew nothing else. I was a clown, my dreams had come true, and I still held the shard of glass.

Sideshow

Carnival Carnage
Samie Sands

God damn 4th of July. It's such a farce!

Every year it's the same old tosh. We have this massive celebration which begins with all the nearby family coming around to ours for a barbeque at lunchtime. This is followed by a good couple of hours with us all pretending not to *totally* hate each other like we do the rest of the year. Then, when all the adults are suitably drunk and things *could* descend into chaos, we pack up and head out to the carnival in the town square.

That bit actually has the potential to be quite fun, if I didn't have to spend the time babysitting my two bratty five-year-old cousins Jack and Jill (nope, not even kidding! Who calls twins such ridiculous names?) and hang about with Daniel. He's the same age as me, but *such* a loser. He loves all sorts of geeky shit and just has absolutely zero social skills. I do *not* know what he does with his time. Luckily, we don't go to the same school. He's far too embarrassing to have around my mates, so I end up spending most of the time trying to avoid everyone I know.

Don't judge me, I actually have a *good* reputation around here, but as we all know, popularity is a fragile thing. Hard to build up, but any little thing can knock you right off the social ladder, straight back down to the bottom. I refuse to have that happen because of my idiot family.

If I'm totally honest, the worst thing of it all is that my bloody mother *always*, without fail, forced me to wear a dress. I have to "Look like a girl for once". She is so God damn old fashioned. People don't wear dresses anymore—that's why jeans were invented for Christ sake! I stare at my unfamiliar reflection and huff, tugging at the hem uncomfortably. This just isn't me in any way. I need this day over with so I can go back to my real life.

Mid-morning brings with it a flurry or grandparents, aunties, uncles, cousins. I can't even begin to keep track. I keep the fake smile plastered across my face, even though inside I am screaming profanities and cringing. The afternoon passes slowly, *very* slowly, but without too much drama. It's surprising really, that all these people can bear to be around each other. After all, they spend the rest of their time bickering over money, child rearing and other pathetic issues. Why must they pretend now? It's so dumb. I'll never understand the politics of adulthood.

The television blares out the political speeches—another 4th July tradition, but I tune out, unable to bear listening. This day is dragging on and I feel so uncomfortable in the swishy, short dress it's unreal. The station finally flickers onto the news, and mum immediately silences it. As I watch the fading black, the inane chatter starts surrounding me again. Why is it that when adults get drunk, they just get louder and more stupid? Seems absolutely ridiculous to me, which is why alcohol has never tempted me.

I finally free myself to shove on some jeans and a plain t-shirt, as we are getting ready to leave for the carnival. The whole facade is embarrassing enough, without being seen in a dress. My parents are suitably out of it now, so I guess they'll never notice. The walk to the carnival is as awful as expected, the twins are screaming top note and running riot around me, and Daniel is blabbering on about Star Trek or Star Wars or something else I don't understand. They're all driving me nuts; I'm just about at the end of my tether. Glancing down at my watch, I can't help but wonder how much longer do I have to suffer this?

Before I know it, the familiar carnival music is blaring out so loud; I know we must only be moments away. I feel a sense of foreboding as I turn the last corner, almost as if I can sense something bad is going to happen. And then predictably, it does. I run smack into Kelly who is lip-locked with Kyle.

I'm too stunned to be humiliated, too angry to move. Kelly is my friend, my *closest* friend. I mean, I've always known that she was untrustworthy, we popular girls normally are, we have to be to survive the jungle of high school, but to do this? She knows how long I have been after Kyle—I have literally liked him forever.

"Bitch!" I spit the accusatory word out before I can regain control of myself before I realize that I am supposed to be incognito. A loud gasp followed by giggling ensures the knowledge that the twins have heard the profanity. I spin around to see them in fits of hysterics, with Daniel blushing brightly. I am too full of rage to think rationally. All I can focus on is a red mist that has descended around me. Kelly and Kyle have pulled apart.

At least they both have the decency to look embarrassed, but the wetness of their lips is too insulting for me to feel any forgiveness.

Angry tears sting my eyes, but I pinch my nose to stop them falling. I refuse to let them have that effect on me.

Sideshow

Kelly starts stammering, explaining, but I can't help but notice she doesn't let go of Kyle's hand even once. He keeps a smug grin on his face the entire time. Why do boys enjoy girls fighting over them so much? It's just weird. I don't want to hear *anything* these two have to say, nothing will make their betrayal less painful, this horrible day any better. I instinctively turn and run off, back the way we came. Away from them, from everyone.

Monday at school is going to be *unbearable*. Any sort of drama draws everyone in, especially a bitch fight between two very popular girls—supposed best friends at that! I can't go through all this crap again. I know it sounds old and boring, but now we're so close to graduating, all I want to do is get my head down, try and achieve something so I can actually go to college. I've started to realize how important this whole education thing is *way* too late, I have so much to catch up on. This is the last thing I need.

I suddenly notice voices and footsteps running behind me. I whirl around, expecting an immediate confrontation with Kelly or Kyle, but no. It's just my cousins. The three people I least want to see in the world. "Just...go back." I pant, trying to stop the steady stream falling from my eyes. "I'll be there in a bit. I just need..." After a few seconds of silence, Daniel pulls me down to sit on the ground. The hardness of the floor pulls me back into reality and the tears become sobs that rack through my entire body.

Finally, I'm pulled out of my self-pity stupor by the twin's concerned chatter. I really shouldn't worry these kids; they don't understand the harsh reality of life yet. They have plenty of time to suffer all that I'm going through. I force a weak smile, and even though all I want to do is go home, I suggest going back to the carnival. I know they'll all want to; sitting with a crying girl will not be in any of their wish lists this holiday.

We walk back, me nervously behind the others. I'm frightened I'm going to see *them* again. One heartbreak a night is enough for me. As we turn the dreaded corner, my heart in my mouth, the sight before me is not what I expected.

High flames. Blackness. Grey smoke.

Everything is on fire. What the fuck is happening? Is this arson? I mean, I know I wasn't exactly looking forward to enduring this hell, but I can't imagine anyone going *this* far. I stand frozen as I watch the firemen shoot jets of water onto the flickering flames, creating more smoke and confusion. Where is everyone? What about the rest of my family? There must be an assembly point somewhere. We should go and find them; they're probably all panicking about us. They've got no idea where we are.

Grabbing hold of the others, we run off. We circle the area, looking for anyone and don't manage to stumble across a solitary soul. I start to feel like I can't breathe. I'm not sure if it's the smoke or the panic. What if everyone died in the flames? Is that possible? That means...

No, forget it. That's just an unbearable thought.

I finally find a fireman to ask. He looks at me confused before shrugging his shoulders, talking quickly and frantically at me in a foreign language. Frustrated, I shout after all of the firemen. But they ignore me, starting to leave. Aren't they supposed to make sure we are safe or something? I walk forward into the black and grey smoldering mess. The others follow I can hear their footsteps and breathing behind me. The twins are whispering to each other. I don't know how much they understand about what's happening and I have no idea how to even begin to explain anything.

Nothing. No one.

I turn to Daniel, my confused expression mirrored in his. What do we do? A noise to my left causes me to spin round. Someone to ask, finally. "Hey!" I call out to the shadowy figure as it moves slowly forward. I shield my eyes, trying to get a clearer view. "Hi, um…We just need some…" I trail off as the person becomes clearer. Kelly. That bitch. She looks a bit banged up, possibly burned, but she's walking around, so must be fine. I turn and stalk off in the opposite direction, refusing to deal with her right now.

The others stay close behind me, obviously unable to make any choices for themselves. Much as they're starting to annoy me, I'm more consumed by relief that at least *someone* else is here. I wish we knew where to find everyone else. I've tried ringing mum, but I guess my network is down. Typical. Phones never seem to work when you need them to most.

The silence rings out, deafening in my ears. My sight is restricted to just in front of me. So, when a loud, high pitched scream, full of terror, pierces the air, it induces immediate terror. "Daniel? Jack? Jill?" I question quietly so as not to disturb the obvious mass murder that is about somewhere, trying to bump everyone in this town off. I push forward, reaching in front of me, trying to hold onto one of them. My hands shoot relief through my body as I touch hair. I almost let out a relieved giggle.

The hair is matted and wet, almost like someone has been swimming in the ocean. It must be Jill, she must have done something when I wasn't looking. I move closer, inhaling. The scent of ash and burnt meat makes me gag, fires seriously stink! I pull Jill in close, inexplicably scared. *Growl.* I snap my head down towards the little girl. Why is she doing that? Suddenly a hot radiating pain takes over, starting in my wrist. I want to scream out, but my mouth feels like it has been sewn shut. I want to move, but my feet feel like lead.

When the mist descends from my eyes, I see a sight before me, which makes no immediate sense, but spells danger to my brain all the same. A woman, not a girl, certainly not Jill, who is covered in blood and pus, her clothes all torn, a bone sticking out from her leg, has her teeth sunk into my arm and seems to be relishing the taste.

I tug my arm back ripping off a chunk of skin as it drags against her mouth, and force my legs to run. I try to block out the pain, try not to let it get to me just yet. Isn't shock supposed to set in at some point, taking over everything else? Distracted, I somehow manage to run smack into a tree, the motion sending me flying back to the ground. The radiating agony in the front of my head blacks everything else out for a single moment.

When I finally come back around, I can feel and see a red sticky liquid running down my face. Blood. Well, that's just great. Just another problem to add to the long list. I look around, confused by the eerie atmosphere. Seriously, this seems like some kind of nightmare. If it weren't for the excruciating pain over all of my body, I could almost let myself believe that this hideous day hadn't even begun yet. That I'm still in my bed. Waiting.

I stagger upright, trying to work out what I should do next. My brain is all...fuzzy. I wish there was some around I could ask for help. If I get back to the smoldering embers of the carnival I might be able to find Daniel or the twins. I think back to my reluctance to be seen with them only hours before, now I'm desperate to see a familiar face, especially one of theirs.

I see in the mist ahead of me, moving shapes. It looks like people, but they're moving weirdly. Sort of jerky and very slowly. I speed on, wanting to find someone, wanting to know what happened here. I reach the group. There are eight people here, but they aren't really...human. They're covered in blood and rot and they smell like gone off barbeque meat. What's with these people? I walk up close to them, wanting an answer. One of them snarls and snaps their teeth at me, before sniffing the air and turning away. I get up in one of the girls faces. Her curious eyes follow me and send shivers up my spine. Her irises are completely white. In fact, all of them look like this. I try and speak to them, but am met with low growls and groans.

They circle around me, staring at me, half disgusted, half curious. I'm sure my expression is the same. One of them is dragging a bloody stump behind him where his leg used to be. He doesn't even seem bothered by this. Nor does the girl who has an obvious stab wound in her stomach—that must hurt like hell. She must be all sorts of tough!

Suddenly a gunshot rings out in the distance. As my head snaps around, searching for help, so does all of theirs. Quickly they are ambling away, any interest in me waning. I follow behind, unsure of what else to do. At least they might lead me somewhere safe. Twelve more gunshots ring out, keeping us all on the right track. I wonder what the significance of the thirteen shots is. A boring history lesson flicks into my mind, somehow familiar, but it is gone before any particular memory can click into place.

As we amble, I can feel my body getting heavier, my mind getting more sluggish, my emotions becoming null and void. What is happening to me? The bite mark on my wrist has, somewhere along the line, turned completely and utterly black—what does that mean? I think I need to get to the hospital. I don't panic though like I normally would. In fact, I feel weirdly serene.

A noise distracts my trail of thoughts. I look up to see the group I was following, all knelt to the ground looking at something. I move in closer, curiosity getting the best of me. I quickly see blood splattering everywhere, which confuses and intrigues me equally.

Vomit fills my mouth when I realize exactly what they're doing. They're *eating* someone. Cannibals. That could quite easily have been me. These people are sickoes. Unless, could this be some kind of zombie apocalypse prank? I think I remember someone doing that in the UK a while ago; someone won a few million on the lottery and created a zombie-infested town to trick his mates. Is this what's happening? Then why did I get bitten, that's a bit much, isn't it? Weirdo! Why aren't I in on the prank? I wish I knew for certain because everything is getting a bit much for me now. All I want to do is cry—and that isn't like me at all.

***

I feel like I haven't seen anyone for days. I have no idea how long I've been wandering about but my emotions are flicking rapidly between despair and frustration. I need some help. I've got to find Daniel and the twins at least. Then we can all head home to see if we can find the rest of our family. Then I'm going to sleep this shitty day off once and for all. Next year I'm not doing a single thing to celebrate 4th July. I'm staying indoors, locked in my room.

Sideshow

I slump down onto a rock, my body refusing to carry on. I think I must sleep or blackout. I have no idea how long for, but when I awaken, the sight before me pushes my mind to its very limit. A dead body lies at my feet. I push back, eyes flicking around, worrying about my own life. Why would those cannibals have eaten this guy and not me? In my haste to move, I nick my wrists, causing black goo to seep from the wound. Could it be this that stopped them? A newfound gratefulness for the woman that bit me overtakes.

I move away as fast as my ailing body will let me. But as I'm going, something inside me shifts, a new emotion takes over. It's hard to describe, even to myself. It sort of feels like a blinding, blackout rage. Suddenly, I don't want to run anymore. I want to stop, to turn, to fight. I don't though because I know it isn't rational, my brain is at least allowing me that much common sense. I keep running until I come across an unusual, intriguing sight.

People. Hundreds of them, all crying, wrapped in blankets, some burnt, badly hurt. Instead of feeling sad, like I know I should, or happy that I'm no longer alone, I feel a rush of something different. Excitement? Lust? Before I know it, I'm charging forwards, bearing my teeth. I don't care anymore about what is right and wrong, all I want to do is copy the cannibals and feel some flesh against my teeth. It's not hunger driving me, more a desire to cause harm, pain, to inflict fear. I want all the people to be pushed to the brink of despair. I want them to experience emotions they didn't even know they could feel.

A loud scream explodes and people fly in every direction. I am slower than them, but the fear I inflict stiffens some of them, allowing me to grab hold. Sinking my teeth into tissue at every opportunity, a rush of euphoria running through me every single time, just to chew on it and spit it out. Once I have bitten a person, they become nothing to me. I have no further use for them, so I toss them aside onto the next.

I hear a voice; it's calling out a name. A stirring of recognition inside causes me to stop. Is that...my name? I turn, feeling a sense of déjà vu, of familiarity, blood dripping down my chin. A group of people behind me, all nervously stepping in my direction, chattering incessantly.

My family. I look at them curiously. What are they doing? I edge closer to them and they rile backward, afraid I realize. They don't need to be frightened of me - I know I attacked others, but I love them, I wouldn't do it to them. Good old Daniel bravely comes closer, the twins cowering behind. He's speaking to me, but I am too transfixed on the saliva glistening on his lips to hear any words. His arms outstretched, wishing me forwards. I step, willing myself to play this cool. If I'm ok with Daniel, the others will trust me and accept me again.

I lean into him, nestling into his chest, breathing in his familiar scent. I smile as I eventually pull back, pleased with myself. I have proved that I can do this. It's only when I stare into Daniel's tearful eyes, his open mouth, that the familiar metallic scent of blood wafts into my nostrils. I realize I have a massive chunk of his neck in my mouth. He falls to the floor, the weight of his body too much. The others run away bellowing out screams. I spit the dirty flesh on the ground. That moment was a game changer. Now all I can focus on is my need to devour them all.

***

Sideshow

Hours later, everyone in the entire town is either an unfortunate casualty or just another member of the shuffling army that I seem to be leading. I don't know why everyone has turned to me, but I am relishing the power and position. Almost as if it's my destiny to be in charge. I look around and try to grin at the familiar faces I have spent the day with, including many members of my delightful family, but my jaw is slack and destroyed from the battle.

We move forward slowly, but with avid determination. None of us know exactly what happened to our little town carnival this Independence Day, no one is even sure why we're like this. The only thing we collectively know now, is there are no humans left here for us to infect, to recruit. We need to move on; we need to take over the next place. Nothing will stand in our way.

Made in the USA
Middletown, DE
30 December 2018